"I don't ~~~~ **you.**

"I thought you wanted my advice," Mark replied.

She fisted her hands on her hips. "You thought wrong. Since you seem to know so much about business, why don't you come up with a plan that will work."

"For you?"

"*Ja*, for me. I'd like to see you figure out everything I need to do to turn a profit. Since you are a furniture maker and not a baker, I don't believe you can do any better than I did."

"It would be difficult to do worse."

Helen made that huffing sound that told him he should've stopped talking a while back. She took the dog's lead from Mark's hand. "Thank you for escorting me home. Good night."

"I'll do it," Mark blurted.

"What?"

"I'll come up with a business plan for you," he said, wondering why he felt compelled to help someone who clearly didn't want it.

"Don't bother." Helen tugged Clyde up the porch steps.

"It's no bother."

But she entered the house and shut the door without answering.

After thirty-five years as a nurse, **Patricia Davids** hung up her stethoscope to become a full-time writer. She enjoys spending her free time visiting her grandchildren, doing some long-overdue yard work and traveling to research her story locations. She resides in Wichita, Kansas. Pat always enjoys hearing from her readers. You can visit her online at patriciadavids.com.

Books by Patricia Davids

Love Inspired

The Amish Bachelors

An Amish Harvest
An Amish Noel
His Amish Teacher
Their Pretend Amish Courtship
Amish Christmas Twins
An Unexpected Amish Romance

Lancaster Courtships

The Amish Midwife

Brides of Amish Country

Plain Admirer
Amish Christmas Joy
The Shepherd's Bride
The Amish Nanny
An Amish Family Christmas: A Plain Holiday
An Amish Christmas Journey
Amish Redemption

Visit the Author Profile page at Harlequin.com for more titles.

An Unexpected Amish Romance

Patricia Davids

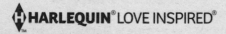

HARLEQUIN® LOVE INSPIRED®

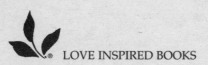 LOVE INSPIRED BOOKS

ISBN-13: 978-1-335-42792-2

An Unexpected Amish Romance

Copyright © 2018 by Patricia MacDonald

www.Harlequin.com

Printed in U.S.A.

Whoso findeth a wife findeth a good thing,
and obtaineth favour of the Lord.
—*Proverbs* 18:22

This book is dedicated with boundless love to my granddaughter Shantel Widick. You are a smart, beautiful young woman of many talents, a lover of animals, a keen-eyed photographer and the person I most enjoy laughing with on a late-night sleepover. Remember to put down the phone and experience life firsthand. Oh, and never drive the four-wheeler that fast in front of your great-grandfather again. Ever.

Love you always.

MeMa Pat

Chapter One

Mark Bowman lifted his straw hat off his face and sat up with a disgruntled sigh. Trying to sleep on a bus was hard enough, but the sound of muffled weeping coming from the seat behind him was making it impossible. He turned to look over his shoulder. The culprit was an Amish woman with her face buried in a large white handkerchief. She was alone. Should he say something or ignore her?

Normally he avoided meddling in the affairs of others, but he recalled his uncle's advice to him before he'd left Bowmans Crossing four days ago. A business owner needed to be a good listener as well as a good salesman. Success wasn't always about numbers, it was about making people feel you cared about them and their concerns. It was about build-

ing friendships. Isaac had asked Mark to make
an effort to be more outgoing on this trip.

There was no one Mark respected more
than his uncle. Isaac Bowman had achieved
everything Mark was working toward. He had
a successful furniture-making business and a
large happy family. Isaac was well respected
in his Amish church and in the community
and with good reason. He was always willing to lend a helping hand.

Mark didn't have to imagine what his uncle
would do in this situation. He would ask if he
could help. Taking a deep breath, Mark spoke
softly to the woman. "Fräulein, are you all
right?"

She glanced up and then turned her face to
the window. "I'm fine."

It was dark outside. There was nothing
to see except the occasional lights from the
farms they passed. She dabbed her eyes and
sniffled. She was a lovely woman. Her pale
blond hair was tucked neatly beneath a gauzy,
heart-shaped white *kapp*. He didn't recognize
the style and wondered where she was from.
"You don't sound fine."

"Maybe not yet, but I will be."

The defiance in her tone took him by surprise and reminded him of his six-year-old
sister when she didn't get her way. Experi-

ence had taught him the best way to stop his sister's tears was to distract her. "I don't care much for bus rides. Makes me queasy in the stomach. How about you?"

"They don't bother me."

"Where are you headed?"

"To visit family." The woman's clipped reply said she wasn't interested in talking about it. He should have let it go at that, but he didn't.

"Then someone in your family must be ill. Or perhaps you are on your way to a funeral."

She frowned at him. "Why do you say that?"

"It's a reasonable assumption. You'd hardly be crying if you were on your way to a wedding."

Tears welled up in her eyes and spilled down her cheeks. With a strangled cry, she scrambled out of her seat and moved to one at the rear of the bus, effectively ending their conversation.

Confused, he stared at her. Somehow he'd made things worse, and he had no idea what he'd said that upset her so. He shook his head in bewilderment. Women could be so unpredictable. Fortunately, the woman he planned to marry was sensible and level-headed. He couldn't imagine Angela drawing attention to herself by weeping in public.

He noticed a few of the nearby passengers scowling at him. He shrugged and settled back to finish his nap. He should have gone with his first instinct to mind his own business. His brother Paul claimed most women were emotional creatures who enjoyed drama and making mountains out of molehills. Clearly she was one of those. He was fortunate she had moved to the back of the bus and wouldn't trouble him again.

Helen Zook squeezed her eyes shut to stem the flow of fresh tears brought on by her nosy and insensitive fellow passenger. His beardless cheeks told her he was a single man. She didn't want to talk to anyone, let alone a handsome dark-haired Amish fellow who was brash enough to strike up a conversation with a woman traveling alone. Perhaps he had meant to be kind, but his words stung. He was half right. She wasn't going to a wedding. She was running away from one.

Today should have been her wedding day, but all her dreams of the happy life ahead of her had come crashing down when her fiancé announced three weeks ago that he had changed his mind. He wanted to marry her sister Olivia instead. Today had been their wedding day.

How could Joseph betray her like that? How could her own sister deceive her by seeing Joseph behind her back? They were questions without answers that tumbled around in her mind like leaves in a whirlwind. Helen refused to admit that some of the blame rested squarely on her shoulders. She was the victim.

The shock and the shame had been more than Helen could bear, although she tried to pretend it didn't matter. She was so angry with them. That was wrong. She knew it, but she couldn't change how she felt. The two people she trusted most in the world had betrayed her and made her a laughingstock in the community.

The morning of her sister's wedding, Helen had realized she couldn't remain at home and watch Olivia wed Joseph. Without a clear idea of what she was going to do, she'd taken her savings and purchased a one-way bus ticket out of Nappanee, Indiana, with the intention of staying with her aunt Charlotte. She hoped she could find a job and get a place of her own soon. She prayed her aunt would take her in. She hadn't had time to write and explain that she was coming nor had she told anyone where she was going.

Helen had met her father's youngest sister a few times over the years when they came to visit at Christmas and such, but she didn't know her aunt well. Charlotte was something of an odd recluse and not overly fond of visitors, but Helen would make herself useful. She was fleeing to her aunt's home because Charlotte lived the farthest away of any of the relatives. She had never married, choosing to stay at home and care for her aging parents until they were both gone. She had a small income from the rental of farmland her father had left her near Bowmans Crossing, Ohio. According to the letters she wrote to Helen's parents, she lived happily with only her pets in a little house by the river.

It seemed like the perfect hideaway to Helen, but as the miles flew by she was learning distance alone didn't diminish a heartache.

Mark roused as the bus slowed and jolted to a halt. "Berlin, Ohio," the driver announced over the intercom. He opened the door with a loud whoosh.

Mark stretched and rose to his feet. After pulling his duffel bag from the overhead bin, he made his way down the aisle and got off the bus. It would be wonderful to sleep in his own bed after having stayed in motels for the past four days, but at least his trip had been a success. He looked forward to telling his uncle that they had two new stores in Columbus willing to sell the handmade furniture produced in his workshop.

Berlin didn't have an actual bus station. They had stopped in a parking lot in front a local restaurant that was already closed for the evening. A single floodlight provided the only illumination, with moths and other insects fluttering around it.

Several other Amish passengers got off the bus including the weeping woman who seemed to have recovered her composure. She pointedly avoided looking at Mark and kept her eyes downcast. There were several buggies parked along the roadway. Various passengers gravitated to them. The woman spoke to the bus driver, who was unloading luggage. He pointed toward a white van at the edge of the parking lot. She nodded and crossed to the vehicle where she spoke to someone inside and then got in.

Not much more than a wide spot in the road, the village of Berlin was still fifteen miles from Mark's destination of Bowmans Crossing. He looked around for his uncle or one of his cousins but didn't see them. They knew he was coming in on this bus, so he expected they would be along soon.

The driver of the white van approached. Mark recognized Abner Stutzman. The wiry gray-haired man was one his uncle's English neighbors who earned extra money by providing taxi service to the Amish folks in the community.

"Evening, Mark."

"*Guten nacht*, Abner."

"Your uncle arranged for me to pick you up and take you home tonight."

Mark grinned. That meant he'd reach his bed all the sooner. "I'm grateful for Onkel Isaac's thoughtfulness."

"I hope you don't mind me taking on another fare. There's a young lady needing a ride, too. She's going past Bowmans Crossing, so it won't hold you up any."

"That's fine." Mark hoped she wouldn't start crying again when she saw he was sharing her ride.

Abner rubbed his hands together. "Okay, let's get going. The missus came along to keep me company, but she doesn't like to stay out late."

Since Abner's wife was seated up front, Mark had no choice but to get in the back. The woman from the bus was already seated in the second row. He had the option of sitting beside her or behind her in the third row of seats. Would she start crying again if he sat beside her? Riding in the back of Abner's van might trigger Mark's motion sickness. Which would be worse? He put his duffel bag on the rear seats and sat down beside her without a word. She kept her face averted.

"All set?" Abner asked, looking at them in the rearview mirror.

The woman nodded slightly. Mark said, "We're ready."

Abner pulled out of the parking lot and onto the narrow highway headed toward Bowmans Crossing. After a few long minutes of awkward silence, Mark decided perhaps he should apologize. He leaned toward her. "I'm sorry I upset you earlier."

"It wasn't you," she murmured. He had to strain to hear her.

She kept her face turned toward the window. He wished he could see her better. "*Goot.* I'd hate to think I added to your troubles."

"You didn't." Her clipped reply wasn't encouraging.

"If no one is ill or has died, why were you crying?"

"My reasons are my own."

He shifted uncomfortably on the seat, feeling out of his depth but sure that his uncle would want him to try and aid her. "Some people say it helps to talk about your problems."

"Well, some people are wrong."

He sighed inwardly with relief. She didn't want to pour out her troubles any more than he wanted to hear them. "I find that's true. I'm glad you don't wish to discuss it with me."

Her eyes widened. "Then why did you offer?"

"My *onkel* tells me I need to work on my communication skills. He says it's important for a business owner. I'm supposed to practice showing interest in people and become a better listener."

"So you chose me to practice on?"

He caught a hint of anger in her tone. "No need to ruffle your feathers."

"My *feathers* are not ruffled," she said through gritted teeth, her eyes snapping with irritation.

"I'd say they are getting more ruffled by the second."

"You are a rude man. We're done talking." She folded her arms tightly across her chest and turned back to the window.

She had no idea how glad he was to hear her say that. Still, he couldn't help wondering what had made her cry in the first place. She stirred his curiosity, and that was unusual.

Twenty-five silent minutes later, Abner pulled to a stop in front of Mark's uncle's home. Mark tipped his hat to the woman and got out. She didn't even glance his way. To his mind, she was the one being rude.

His uncle's advice was harder to put into practice than he expected it to be.

The following day, Mark stayed busy in his uncle's workshop until early evening. Although he had been put in charge by his uncle and oversaw the day-to-day operations of the business, it was carving that Mark enjoyed the most. He was putting the finishing touches on a mantelpiece depicting foxes at play in the woods when his uncle stopped beside him.

As Mark had hoped, his uncle had been pleased with the success of his trip. He had omitted telling him about the woman on the bus, although he wasn't sure why. Maybe it was because he hadn't been successful in that endeavor. He kept going over their conversations trying to pinpoint what he'd done wrong, but he couldn't put his finger on it.

"Time to close up shop, Mark. Ah, I see you're almost done with the mantel. This is *goot* work. If you decide not to open your own business, I'd be happy to keep you on here. You have a rare God-given talent."

"*Danki*, but I will stick to my plan."

"I felt sure you would say that. Don't let your supper get cold."

"I'll be along in a few minutes." Mark ran his hand along the surface of his project, satisfied with the way it had turned out. All that was left was to stain the oak wood the color the customer wanted. It was one of his better pieces, although he was a long way from being a master carver the way his cousin Samuel and coworker Adam Knepp were.

A short time later, he entered the front door of his uncle's home and saw his brother, Paul, waiting with a big grin on his face.

"Your fair Angela has written you another love letter, *bruder*. Will you read it aloud to us tonight?"

Mark ignored his brother and picked up the letter addressed to him from the top of the mail piled on the end of the kitchen counter. Despite his foolish younger brother's suggestion, Mark knew it wasn't a love letter. Angela was too practical for such nonsense. Their relationship was based on respect and the knowledge that their marriage would be mutually beneficial to both their families.

He slipped the letter into his pocket to read

later and hung his straw hat on one of the pegs by the kitchen door. Seven identical Amish hats were already lined up. His uncle, his five cousins and his brother had come in earlier. Mark had lingered behind making sure the lights were off in the workshop, checking on the orders for the next workday and making certain the generator had enough fuel to start up again when they needed it. His uncle had placed Mark in charge of the business for the last three months of his apprenticeship. He was determined to show his uncle his faith wasn't misplaced.

"Leave off teasing Mark and sit down for supper," Anna Bowman said, carrying a steaming pot of roast beef and vegetables to the kitchen table using her folded black apron as a hot pad for her hands.

"I can't leave off teasing him, Aenti Anna. It's *Gott's* will that I annoy my big brother since Mark annoys the rest of us. He has become a tyrant."

"I never ask anyone to do more than I can do myself." Mark pulled out a chair and took his place at the long table. His uncle Isaac sat at the head of the table with his oldest son, Samuel, at his right hand. The rest of Isaac's sons were arranged according to age down the length of the table with Mark and Paul taking up the last two chairs. The wives and daughters of Mark's cousins were seated on the opposite side, all in plain Amish dresses with their black work aprons and white prayer *kapps*. It made a big family gathering when everyone was home. The room was filled with chatter and the clinking of dishes along with the pleasant aromas of the stew, cornbread muffins and hot coffee.

Anna surveyed the table and then took her place at the foot. The noise died away. Isaac bowed his head, and everyone did the same, reciting the blessing in silence. When Isaac raised his head, signaling the prayer was finished, the business turned to eating. The talk was minimal until the meal was over.

After finishing his peach cobbler, Isaac leaned back in his chair and patted his stomach. "It was a *goot* meal."

"*Danki*, husband. What time do you expect to start the frolic in the morning?"

"I imagine most workers will be here by eight o'clock as long as the rain holds off."

All the members of the Bowman family had arrived to help with the work party set for the following day. The women had spent the day cooking and cleaning since Isaac and Anna were hosting the party. Most of their Amish community would come to help clear the log-jam beneath the only bridge into and out of the valley on the far side of the river. While the men worked, the women would usually visit then serve coffee and a hearty lunch, but tomorrow there was to be a quilting party for the women, too. As the rest of the men went into the living room, leaving the women to clean up, Mark went upstairs to his room at the back of the house.

His window was open, and the evening breeze fluttered the simple white curtains his aunt had in all the upstairs bedrooms. Outside, the spreading branches of a huge ancient silver maple tree kept the room cool, but it obstructed the view of the river from this room. Mark didn't mind. It was more practical to have a cool place to sleep in the summer than a view.

His uncle had been talking about cutting the tree down. The old thing was past its prime, having as many dead limbs as live ones branching off its enormous trunk. Silver maples were notorious for breaking in wind storms. Two large limbs had come down in the last storm, fortunately on the side away from the house, but it was only a matter of time before one fell on the roof. Mark's aunt was the reason the tree hadn't been taken down already. She had an irrational, sentimental attachment to it because Isaac's parents had planted it the year Isaac was born.

Mark pulled out his letter and sat on the edge of his bed. Angela's letters came like clockwork every Tuesday, and today was no exception. She normally wrote about the weather and the people back home, about her father's lumber milling business and about what changes she hoped to make to the farm when she and Mark were married. Unlike with the overly emotional woman on the bus, he knew exactly what to expect from Angela.

His letters to her were about his work and the ways he saw he could incorporate his uncle's teachings into the business he would own one day. The day was fast approaching when he could put his plan into effect.

It had been her father's business and the location of their farm that first gave Mark the idea to build his future workshop there. Otis Yoder's small farm had poor, rocky soil, but it fronted a busy road in an area where tourists flocked to gawk at Amish folks and buy Amish-made goods. The fact that Otis could supply almost all the raw lumber Mark would need cinched the plan in his mind.

When Mark had approached Otis about buying some of his land, Otis wasn't interested. He saw value in Mark's idea but wanted his farm and business to go to Angela, his only child. Mark persisted, and eventually Otis made a surprising counteroffer. If Mark would marry Angela, then Otis would enter a partnership with him. Angela was a widow a few years older than Mark. She was quiet, hardworking and practical. To his amazement, she agreed with her father's proposal.

Getting a wife along with the land was a bonus in Mark's eyes. He'd never had the time or the inclination to date women, but he did want a family one day. He wanted sons to carry on the business he would build. The idea of romance and falling in love to achieve that didn't make sense. Why base one of the most important decisions a man could make on something as flimsy as a feeling? In his mind, it was much better to base it on mutual respect and shared goals than love.

He and Angela had settled on a long-distance courtship while Mark apprenticed with his uncle. Mark sent her a portion of his paychecks each month as a down payment on the land.

Little by little he had been accumulating the machinery and tools he would need and had them stored in his father's barn not far from the Yoder farm. Isaac had put him in contact with people who were interested in purchasing Pennsylvania Amish–made furniture. Things were almost ready for him to open his business.

He slipped his finger under the envelope flap and tore it open. He quickly skimmed through her short letter. It didn't contain any of the usual news. Mark couldn't believe his eyes. He read the note again. Angela wanted to end their engagement.

For almost two years he had been working toward a goal that would provide them with a lifetime of security and now, two months before he was due to return home, she was tired of waiting for him?

They had talked about this before he left, and she had assured him that two years would pass before they knew it. Angela agreed they had to stick to a plan if they were going to succeed. He read her words again. She was sorry, but she no longer wished to marry him.

What was the plan now? What about the land? What about his partnership with her father? What about the money he'd sent? He had no idea where all of that stood. He crumpled the note into a ball and threw it toward the wastebasket in the corner. It bounced off the rim.

The door opened, and Paul stuck his head

in. "What did the fair Angela have to say? Did she send you a hug and kiss with an *x* and *o* ?"

"My business is my own, Paul," Mark snapped. He wasn't ready to share this news, certainly not with Paul.

"Hey, you look a little funny. Is something wrong?" Paul took a step into the room.

"Your harassment is what's wrong. I'm tired of your jabs."

Paul held up both hands. "*Bruder*, I never mean you harm. I hope you know that. Forgive me if I have offended you."

Mark rose from the bed. "Please forgive me also. I'm tired tonight, that's all."

He took Paul by the shoulders and turned him to the door. "I need my sleep and so do you. We'll have a hard day tomorrow."

"You might. I intend to have fun."

"When do you have anything else?" Mark gave him a friendly shove out into the hall and closed the door behind him. He bent to pick up the crumpled letter. Instead of throwing it into the trash, he smoothed it out. He had planned a future with her for so long that he wasn't sure how to plan one without her.

If she didn't want to marry him, that was fine, but what about the land? All she said was that her feelings toward him had changed. How was that possible if they hadn't seen each other? Although their intentions hadn't been made public, he saw her request as a breach of contract. With a few strokes of her pen she upset his carefully thought-out plan and left him twirling in the wind like a new-fallen leaf.

He needed to consider all the ramifications of what this meant. He didn't have enough information. He sat down to write and ask for more details. Even if Angela's father still intended to sell Mark the land, he now faced the distasteful task of finding another woman to marry. In his opinion, courting was a waste of a man's time.

Unbidden, the memory of the woman from the bus slipped into his mind. She was the perfect example of why he dreaded looking for a mate. All he had done was try to help. In the first instance, his words had sent her fleeing in tears. In the second, they had made her spitting mad, and he still had no idea why.

Who was she? Why had she been crying? Abner had said she was going beyond Bowmans Crossing. The chances of seeing her again were slim.

So why couldn't he get her tear-stained face out of his head?

Chapter Two

Two days after arriving unannounced at her aunt's home outside of Bowmans Crossing, Helen Zook sat in the buggy beside her aunt Charlotte wishing she had thought to plug her ears with cotton before leaving the house. The woman had been talking nonstop for the past two miles. Her basset hound had been barking loudly for almost as long.

"Remember, Helen, as far as anyone knows, you are here to visit me for the summer. The less said about your unfortunate incident, the better. In fact, don't say anything about it. Unless you are specifically asked, then you mustn't lie. Liars never prosper."

"It's cheaters."

"What did you say, Helen? Clyde, do be quiet."

"I said cheaters never prosper."

"Of course they don't. I'm sure you have never cheated anyone. I know I haven't. The truth is the best defense, Helen, but there's no point in telling people everything. Bowmans Crossing is a wonderful community, but there are those among us who like to spread gossip. I shouldn't name names, but Verna Yoder and Ina Fisher are the worst offenders. Clyde, get down, can't you see I'm driving?"

Charlotte gently pushed aside the overweight brown-and-white hound dog trying to climb onto her lap. Helen took him by the collar and tugged him back to the floor. He gave her a mournful look before settling all seventy pounds of his wrinkles and flab on her left foot. Gritting her teeth, Helen tried to move him, but he refused to budge another inch.

Charlotte slowed the horse as the buggy rounded the curve beside the district's one-room school. The playground and swings were empty now. The students were home for the summer, but Helen couldn't go home.

"Are you paying attention to me, dear? I feel as if I'm talking to myself."

Helen freed her foot, but her shoe remained under Clyde's slobbery chin. "I'm paying attention, Aenti Charlotte. I'm visiting for the summer. Don't mention that my fiancé humiliated me in front of all our family and friends when he threw me over because he wanted to marry my sister *one week* before the banns for our wedding were to be announced. Bowmans Crossing is wonderful, except for the gossiping pair Ina Fisher and Verna Yoder. Cheaters never prosper, but they can get married and live happily ever after, but I don't have to watch them moon over each other. How could my own sister do this to me? How could Joseph?"

Helen didn't share the part she had played in the disaster. Why should she? She was the one suffering now.

It was all so horrible. She might have been able to bear the pitying looks and well-meaning comments that only served as salt in the wound. The real thing she couldn't tolerate was seeing how happy they were together.

"You girls will make up, and this will all be forgotten in time."

"I don't see how. She stole the man I wanted to marry." Helen's voice crackled.

Joe should have stood by her. If he loved her, he would have. Helen raised her chin. It was painful, but it was better to know how shallow his affections had been before they wed.

"You must not look at what you have lost

for it is not your will that is important. It is His will."

"His will was to marry my sister, and he did just that."

Charlotte cast Helen a sidelong glance. "I'm not talking about that young man's will. It is *Gott's* will you must accept. You must forgive your sister and her husband as is right."

"I forgive them." Helen spoke the words, but they didn't echo in her heart. The pain was too new and too raw.

"That is *goot*. Forgiving blesses the forgiver as much as the forgiven." Charlotte clicked her tongue to get the horse moving faster.

The road straightened, and a covered bridge came into view. The weathered red wooden structure stood in sharp contrast to the thick green trees that grew along the roadway and along the river in both directions. Wide enough for two lanes of traffic, the opening loomed like a cave. A new community awaited Helen beyond the portal. What would she find? Hopefully employment.

Charlotte pointed with her chin. "Just the other side of the river is Isaac Bowman's home, but you have to go about a quarter of a mile farther down the road and turn the corner to reach their lane. That's where the frolic is being held today. He and his wife, Anna, have five sons. I'm sorry to say the young men have all married, but Isaac has two nephews from Pennsylvania living with him now and they are unwed, although one has a girl back home."

It had been dark when the van stopped to let her rude companion out, but Helen was almost certain the Bowman house had been his destination. They hadn't exchanged names so she couldn't be sure of his identity. She hoped and prayed he wouldn't be at the frolic. Her behavior hadn't been the best but neither had his.

"Isaac also employs a number of unmarried fellows in his furniture-making business. You will have plenty of young men to pick from."

Helen rolled her eyes. "You make it sound like I've arrived at the husband orchard."

"The husband orchard. How cute. It should be the title of a book. I'd read it. Oh, that's very clever."

It hadn't taken Helen long to realize her aunt was an avid reader. Her living room held stacks of dog-lover magazines and heaps of novels, from an extensive collection of the classics to some popular romance stories the bishop might raise an eyebrow at if he knew she had them.

Charlotte chuckled and looked at her dog. "Isn't Helen a clever girl, Clyde?"

He took it as an invitation to climb into his mistress's lap. Helen used the opportunity to grab her damp shoe.

"Not now, Clyde, I'm driving." Charlotte pushed him aside. Helen quickly drew her knees up and wrapped her arms around them to give the hound more room to spread out on the floorboards. He locked gazes with her but didn't test her patience by trying to climb in her lap. Instead, he started barking at the roof. Scrabbling overhead accompanied by a chittering sound proved her aunt's pet raccoon was still safely riding atop the buggy.

"Did we have to bring Juliet?"

"Her feelings would be hurt if I took Clyde along and didn't take her."

"We could have left them both at home." The buggy rolled into the dark interior of the bridge. The horse's hoofbeats echoed back from the rafters. Helen stared through the slatted sides at the Bowman house on the hillside across the river. She could see tables had been set up on the lawn, and groups of people were already gathered there.

"Honestly, Helen, I don't think you like my little friends. Please remember they had made their home with me long before you arrived, and they'll be with me long after you have gone back to Indiana."

"I'm not going back to Indiana." Helen had no idea where she was going, but she would make her own way in the world. As soon as she found the means to support herself.

Charlotte's brow wrinkled with concern. "You are welcome to reside with me for the summer, but you never said anything about staying permanently."

"Don't worry. You won't be burdened with me for long."

"That's the spirit. Things will work out for you and your sister. You'll see. Oh, Clyde won't be happy until he can look out the windshield. Helen, take the reins."

Helen grabbed for the lines her aunt dropped as she scooted over to make room for her dog. The horse veered sharply to the right as they came out of the dark bridge into the bright sunlight. A man standing on the edge of the roadway was forced to jump backward to avoid being run down.

Helen managed to stop the horse. Clyde, now taking up more than his fair share of the front seat, started barking wildly. Helen leaned out the door to look back to see if the man was injured. He appeared unharmed as he got to his feet. "I'm sorry," she called out.

Her breath caught in her throat. The man picking his hat up off the road was the fellow from the bus. She knew by the way his eyes widened that he recognized her, too. His brows snapped together in a fierce frown. "If you can't drive any better than that, you should give the reins to the dog," he shouted at her.

Of all the nerve. As much as Helen wanted to tell him exactly what she thought of his rudeness, she held her tongue for her aunt's sake. It wouldn't do to start her time in Bowmans Crossing by embarrassing Charlotte in front of her friends, for several women were walking along the roadway with hampers and baskets over their arms. The women all waved or called a greeting to Helen's aunt. Charlotte waved Clyde's front paw at them. Helen slapped the reins on the horse's rump, and the mare trotted forward.

"Who was that rude man?" she asked, glancing in her rearview mirror.

Charlotte turned to look behind them. "The one standing by the bridge? That's Mark Bowman. The nephew. He has a girl back home. I admit he's a nice-looking young man with those striking green eyes, but handsome is as handsome is."

"As handsome does," Helen said, glancing back again. He wasn't bad-looking, but she didn't think he was particularly good-looking. Okay, maybe he was mildly attractive.

"As handsome does what, dear?"

Helen took note of her aunt's faintly puzzled expression and sighed inwardly. She'd only been at her aunt's home for two days, but it was already shaping up to be a trial. "Never mind."

"You'd do better to try and attract the attention of the younger brother, Paul, although Anna tells me Mark is the more hardworking of the two."

"I'm not here to attract a man." She wouldn't make that mistake again anytime soon. If ever. And certainly not with a rude, arrogant fellow like Mark Bowman or his brother.

Mark raked a hand through his hair as he stared after the buggy. That had been a close call. If he hadn't been so preoccupied with thoughts of Angela's letter, he might have seen the horse veering his way sooner. It wasn't like him to be distracted. He grew angry with himself for allowing it to happen.

"Are you all right?" His brother, Paul, came up the steep bank, his eyes full of concern. His cousin Noah rushed up behind Paul.

"I thought you were going to be wearing

hoofprints up the front of your shirt. Who was that?" Paul demanded.

"Charlotte Zook," Noah said. "I recognized the raccoon on her roof. The woman is a little *ab en kopp*."

Mark shook his head. "Charlotte may be off in the head, but she wasn't driving. I don't know the woman's name, but I saw her get off the bus when I did the other night." He decided not to share the conversation they'd had.

"Another mystery woman." Paul craned his neck to see down the road.

"What does that mean?" Mark asked.

Paul grinned. "Haven't you heard? We've got nearly a dozen new single girls visiting folks in the area. They are all unknown to me and waiting to be discovered. Was the girl driving Charlotte's buggy pretty?"

His brother was always on the lookout for an attractive girl. He was four years younger than Mark, and he hadn't yet learned that looks didn't matter. A man needed a steady, strong, levelheaded woman for a helpmate. He thought he had that with Angela, but he had been wrong. "I didn't notice. I was trying not to get run down. Let's get this frolic under way."

The *frolic*, a word the Amish used for almost any kind of work party, had been called by Mark's uncle Isaac Bowman to clear a log-jam from beneath the covered bridge. The recent rains and flooding had wedged an unusual amount of debris there, which was acting like a dam. Although the county was responsible for maintaining the bridge, the public works department was swamped with other repairs and couldn't bring in their heavy equipment for another two weeks. With the forecast calling for more rain, flooding could threaten farms and homes on both sides of the river.

Men with chainsaws and teams of horses had been arriving for the past half hour and were now gathering on the roadway. Isaac strode up to Mark and surveyed the men around him.

"I reckon we have all the help we need to get started. I sure appreciate you coming," Isaac said, addressing the group. "Samuel and I will oversee the men pulling logs free and getting them up to the roadway. Noah, Paul and Mark will cut and stack the usable wood beside our barn to be divided among our families. The Lord has supplied us with free firewood for the taking. We shouldn't let it go to waste. My sons Timothy and Luke will flag down vehicles heading for the bridge to warn them we are working here." Both men he spoke of were wearing their volunteer fire-fighter jackets and pants with bright fluorescent yellow banding.

Isaac turned to Mark. "There is more rope in the barn loft. Bring it with you. We may need it." He turned back to the men. "Are there any questions?"

Everyone knew what was expected of them. The group split up, and Mark headed with his brother and his cousin toward his uncle's barn, where the family's draft horses were hitched to two large hay wagons. Noah looked over at Mark. "Aren't you going to miss us?"

Mark knew what he was referring to. "Sure, I'll miss all of you when I leave. Your whole family has been good to me."

"But you won't miss us enough to stay."

"Staying here isn't part of my plan." Mark had learned the business of woodworking and furniture making from the ground up working alongside his uncle and his five cousins, but it was almost time to return home and put his knowledge to use and open his own business. He realized he was more upset about the uncertainty facing him now than he was about Angela's decision not to marry him.

"Plans change," Noah said with a wry smile. Mark knew Noah's desire to play professional baseball had been changed by the neighbor girl across the road. Fannie and Noah had wed last fall.

Paul laid a hand on Mark's shoulder. "My brother's plans don't change. He's been talking about starting his own furniture-making business since he could talk."

"I'm guessing it's the girl back home that has Mark pining to leave us. Fair Angela. Paul, is she fair or is she dark-haired? Mark never talks about her."

"I like to keep my personal life private," Mark said before Paul could comment.

"I can respect that." Noah nodded solemnly but couldn't keep a straight face.

Paul chuckled. "Don't let my brother fool you, Noah. He doesn't have a personal life. With him, it's all work, work, work."

"Hard work and strong faith will supply a man with the best rewards in this life and in the next." They were words Mark believed in.

"But will it put a pretty woman in your arms?" Paul asked, wagging his eyebrows.

Noah chuckled. "Are you ever serious?"

"Not if I can help it. Mark and Angela are the serious ones. I'm not sure I've ever seen them laugh."

Mark scowled at his brother. "Not everyone is a jokester like you."

"Fannie makes me laugh all the time. I love

that about her." Noah's gaze shifted toward the house where the women were working. A gentle smile curved his lips. It was easy to see the newlyweds were still madly in love.

Love was okay for some men, but it took more than that frail emotion to build a future. Mark wanted the security of a home and a business where he could support a family. He never wanted his children shuttled from one temporary home to another the way he had been passed from relative to relative when his father was out of work. God willing, Mark's younger sisters and his children would never know the kind of fear he had known wondering if his father would come back for him each time he left.

Mark glanced back toward the bridge. The first logs were already on the roadway. "We should get moving. They have started without us. Where is the extra rope?"

He wouldn't tell his brother and his cousins about Angela today. He'd wait until he knew exactly where he stood with her father.

A quarter mile past the bridge, Helen and her aunt reached the stop sign on the main road between Berlin and Winesburg. An enormous oak tree stood near the intersection. Dozens of gaily painted gourds hung from its branches. Helen stared at them in amazement. "Look at all the birdhouses. How lovely."

Smiling, Charlotte murmured her agreement. "Very pretty. I believe Luke Bowman makes them. Turn here, dear. The Bowman lane is up ahead."

A sign proclaiming Amish-made gifts and crafts fronted the highway in front of a low blue building. There were several cars and buggies in the parking lot dotted with mud puddles left over from the recent rain. Helen glanced at her aunt. "Do the Bowmans run a gift shop?"

"Anna does. Isaac runs the woodworking business in that building up ahead. He employs almost two dozen young men along with his sons. He ships his furniture to *Englisch* businesses across several states. I understand his work is much in demand. The community is grateful for his efforts to keep our young men employed, since not all of them can farm these days."

It was a common problem in many Amish communities. Cottage industries were needed where farmland was too expensive, or urban encroachment had gobbled up land that once supported small farms. "Does Isaac hire women in his factory?"

Helen needed a way to support herself.

She'd been serious when she said she wasn't going home.

"I believe he has hired one or two for office work."

"Full-time jobs?" Helen didn't know anything about woodworking, but she was willing to learn.

Charlotte shook her head. "I don't think so."

Helen eyed the gift shop. Maybe she could find employment there. She had worked in a fabric store for a while back home. She had retail experience.

"Park by the barn, Helen, and try to stay out of the mud. Clyde loves it. I'm delighted you will have a chance to meet so many people at this frolic. I do enjoy them, but sometimes I feel guilty visiting with my friends while we watch the men work."

The grounds were dotted with puddles, but Helen saw a dry place to let her aunt get out. She drew the horse to stop. "Aenti, you and I have been up baking since before dawn. We have already done our work. I hope the men know it."

"How could they? I wouldn't want a bunch of men watching me at work in my kitchen. It's much too small. I guess they could stand outside and look in the window."

Helen sent up a quick prayer for a job and a place of her own as soon as possible.

Her aunt took Clyde's face between her hands. "I'm sorry, dear friend, but you are going to have to stay on your leash until you calm down and mind your manners. I can't have you jumping on everyone you see. Helen is going to look after you. I'll take the hamper to the house."

Helen got out, keeping a tight hold on the dog's leash after noting his interest in the puddles. She glanced at the buggy top. "What about Juliet?"

Charlotte put the hamper down and stepped back to survey the top of the buggy. "Come here, dear one. She doesn't jump on people, so she has no need for a leash."

The plump raccoon scrambled down. A bright pink collar marked her as a pet. Charlotte picked her up and settled her in the crook of her arm, where she began purring loudly. After a moment, she climbed to the top to Charlotte's shoulder and began patting her face and *kapp*.

A trio of women walked past, carrying baskets and boxes. Clyde nearly jerked Helen's arm out of the socket as he tried to leap at them, woofing in his deep tone. Charlotte greeted the woman and walked off with them.

Helen bent to pick up the hamper of baked goods her aunt had left on the ground. As she switched Clyde's leash to her other hand, he spotted a new victim and launched himself at a man stepping out of the barn door, ripping the lead from Helen's hands. Her shriek wasn't enough warning. Clyde hit the man in the back of knees and felled him like a scythed weed. Right into a puddle.

"I'm so sorry." Helen rushed to snag Clyde's leash before he could do more damage. Loud guffaws of laughter erupted from the two men who came to help the poor victim to his feet. When he turned around, Helen wanted to sink into the mud herself. It was Mark Bowman, the rude man from the bus. The one she narrowly missed running down ten minutes ago.

He stood and shook the mud from his hands. His eyes widened when he caught sight of her. "You! I might have known."

"I'm sorry. He got away from me. He's very strong." She pulled Clyde to her side, where he sat happily with his tongue lolling, looking as innocent as only a dog can.

The men with Mark were trying to stifle their laughter without much success. He glared at them and then at her. "Has anyone told you that you're a menace?"

Helen's mouth dropped open. It wasn't like

she had planned to humiliate him. She fisted her hands on her hips. "Let me think. *Nee*, no one has mentioned it, but I'm sure someone has told you that you're judgmental as well as rude."

She spun on her heels and yanked on Clyde's lead. He ambled happily beside her, occasionally stepping on his own long ears.

When she rounded the corner of the house and was sure she couldn't be seen by *him*, she stopped and stared at Clyde. "This was not how I wanted to start out in a new community. I'm going to have to apologize."

She peeked around the corner of the house. Mark was still standing with his friends. She jerked back when he looked her way. She pressed her head against the side of the house. She didn't have the courage to return and face him.

"I don't need to apologize, I just need to avoid him. How hard can that be?"

Chapter Three

Mark stared after the woman as she vanished around the corner of the house. He couldn't remember the last time someone had made him so angry. "I think she did that on purpose. Who is she?"

Paul continued to chuckle. "What did you say that upset the *madel* enough to set her *hund* on you?"

Mark wasn't proud of his earlier comment. "Nothing."

"The truth now, I heard you shout something at her when the buggy flew past you. What did you say, *bruder*?"

"After she almost ran me down, I said if she couldn't drive any better than that to give the reins to the dog."

"Ouch." Noah grimaced.

"I know. It was not my best moment." He

could see now that he'd been too harsh. Both times. He rubbed his hands on his pants. They would be dirtier than this before the day was over anyway. Hopefully, she and her mutt would stay out of his way from now on. He'd sure keep an eye out for the pair. Looking toward the house, he wondered how long she would be staying in the area.

Noah combed his short beard with the fingers of one hand. "She's a good judge of character."

Mark picked up the rope he had dropped. "What makes you say that?"

"I know that you can be judgmental and rude, but I've worked beside you for two years. She's only just met you."

"I'm not judgmental." He looked at his cousin and his brother. "Am I?"

They both nodded. Mark tossed his rope in the wagon. "I like to see things done the right way. Stop laughing like jackals and get to work."

Paul climbed to the wagon seat still chuckling. "I wonder if she will rent out her dog. I'd love to have a way to take you down a peg or two when you get short with me."

"If you did your work, I wouldn't get short with you, and if I never see that mutt again, it will be too soon." Mark hauled himself up beside his brother.

"I like him. He's a cute dog. Fannie adores him." Noah boarded the other wagon and picked up the reins.

"He's a ridiculous animal. His legs are too short, his ears are too big and he smells bad."

Paul unwound the reins from the brake handle. "Careful, your rude and judgmental character is showing."

"Go soak your head." Mark glanced toward the house again, but *she* was staying out of sight. Who was she?

Helen found Anna Bowman directing the placement of tables and benches that would be used when the noonday meal was served. Charlotte was standing beside her. She caught sight of Helen and motioned her over.

Clyde tried jumping on Anna when she came within range, but Helen was prepared and held on tightly.

Charlotte swept a hand toward Helen. "I've brought my niece along. Helen is visiting me for the summer. That's the only reason she is here, and I'm not going to say another word about it."

Anna chuckled. "And a very good reason it is. It's nice to meet you, Helen. I'm Anna

Bowman." She turned and beckoned to a young woman at one of the tables. "Fannie, will you show Helen where we are setting up the food? Fannie is married to my youngest son, Noah. She'll introduce you to everyone and make you feel welcome."

"Oh, I see Grace and Silas Yoder. Let's go say hello, Juliet." Charlotte and Anna walked away to visit with an older woman in a wheelchair and the man standing behind her. The couple called a greeting to Clyde, who barked and wagged his tail.

Her aunt was quickly surrounded by a group of children who wanted a closer look at Juliet. The raccoon seemed delighted with the attention, moving from shoulder to shoulder and patting each child's face in turn.

"Your aunt is quite a character," Fannie said.

Helen judged Fannie to be near her own age. Twenty-two or twenty-three perhaps. She had a contagious smile, red hair and more than her fair share of freckles. She turned aside to avoid Clyde's leap and said, "Bad dog. Sit."

To Helen's amazement, he did. "I don't believe it."

Fannie laughed. "I've had a lot of experience training animals. My husband and I train horses. Let me take the hamper. Where are you from, and how long will you be staying with us?"

"I'm from Nappanee, Indiana, and I'll be staying with Aenti Charlotte until I can find a job and get a place of my own." Helen walked beside Fannie toward the house. Clyde trotted happily at Fannie's side, sending her adoring glances.

"You're planning to settle here permanently?" Fannie walked beneath the branches of a large tree near the door at the rear of the house. She held the door open.

"That will depend on what kind of job I can find. Any suggestions?"

"My husband mentioned something about his father's business needing help the other day, but I don't know any details. What kind of work are you looking for?"

"One that pays a salary. I'm not picky."

"We don't have many businesses in this area. Besides the woodworking shop, there is only Anna's gift shop and a hardware store up the road that's run by Luke Bowman and his wife. I'll introduce you to Emma after we put this food out, but I'm sure they aren't looking for help. Emma has two younger brothers."

Helen followed Fannie to the kitchen and started to unpack her hamper. Clyde raised his nose to sniff the food already laid out on the counters. Fannie put a foot on the leash as he tried to jump up, foiling his effort to snatch a tidbit.

"Down." The single stern word from Fannie made him plop on the floor. She praised him sweetly. He wagged his entire rear end but stayed put.

Through the open kitchen window, Helen could see the operation below the bridge as logs were hauled out. An older man with a long gray beard was directing the operation. Mark Bowman and the two other men Helen had seen earlier stood conferring with him as several of the bigger logs were being hoisted onto a wagon. Why hadn't she kept her mouth shut instead of calling him rude? He must think she was a sharp-tongued woman without an ounce of meekness, and he would be right.

She drew herself up straight. Maybe she was. She didn't have to be meek, but she did have to find work. She studied the older man beside Mark.

"Is that your father-in-law, Isaac Bowman?" Helen would ask him about a job as soon as the opportunity arose.

Fannie glanced out the window. "It is. The good-looking fellow with the short beard is my husband, Noah. The other two with them are Mark and Paul Bowman. They are Isaac's nephews."

"I almost ran into Mark earlier and then Clyde did. It wasn't pleasant."

Fannie grinned and took a step closer. "That sounds intriguing. Do tell."

Something about the sparkle in Fannie's eyes prompted Helen to confide in her. "On our way here, Aenti Charlotte dropped the lines and I grabbed them as we came through the bridge. The horse veered sharply and almost ran into Mark as he stood at the side of the road. He suggested that I let the dog drive if I couldn't do any better."

"He didn't?"

Helen nodded. "He yelled at me."

"Mark can be gruff, but I'm sure he was sorry he shouted at you."

"That wasn't the worst of it. A short time later, Clyde jumped on him from behind and laid him out in a mud puddle in front of your husband and Paul."

Fannie giggled and clapped both hands over her mouth. "That I would have liked to see. Mark is the stuffy sort. It's odd that Clyde should pick on him."

"I haven't noticed that Clyde is particular about who he jumps on."

"He can be. Mark is all business. I imagine

my husband was laughing, but I'll guess that Paul was roaring. He has a...large...sense of humor."

"I was so embarrassed that I barely noticed. Mark was not laughing. He called me a menace."

Fannie smothered her grin. "He shouldn't have done that. He owes you an apology. It was an accident. Everyone knows Clyde isn't exactly well trained." Fannie glanced at the dog lying quietly at her feet.

"I'm afraid I'm the one who owes Mark an apology. I told him he was rude and judgmental, and then I fled."

Repeating her comment aloud made her ashamed of her behavior. She bowed her head. "I'm afraid I showed a serious lack of *demut*."

Fannie slipped an arm around Helen's shoulders and gave her a squeeze. "Humbleness is something I struggle with, too. Don't worry about it. I will say you hit the nail on the head about Mark. Don't get me wrong. I like him, but he's not the friendly sort. He's hardworking, diligent and thrifty, all fine traits, but not much fun. I think underneath there is a happier man waiting to emerge."

Helen appreciated Fannie's understanding and knew she had made her first friend in

Bowmans Crossing. "Would it be forward of me to ask Isaac about a job today?"

"You'll have to ask Mark. Isaac put him in charge of hiring new workers a few months ago."

"Oh, dear." Helen closed her eyes. How much worse could this get? So much for not caring what Mark Bowman thought of her. He wasn't likely to hire her after the way she had spoken to him, even if he had been rude first. "Are you sure you don't know of anyone else looking to hire a maid or a nanny, a gardener, anything?"

"I don't. I'm sorry, but there will be lots of people here today. Maybe someone will have better news for you."

"If you hear of anything, please let me know." If nothing else was available, she would have to apologize and soon. What could she say that would make up for her stinging comments to him?

Fannie lifted a container of pastry from Helen's basket. "These cream horns look yummy. Did you make them?"

"I did. Have one and tell me what you think. It's a new recipe. I've added something special to the puff pastry."

Fannie bit into the cream-filled treat and her eyes widened. "Oh, Helen, these are amazing."

"Danki."

"I hate to admit it, but I'm not much of a cook. I'd rather be taking care of the horses outside instead of doing anything inside."

"Baking is a pleasure, not a chore. I love finding ways to improve on things I've made or try out ways to add different flavors and textures to breads and cakes."

"My mother always told me that the way to man's heart is through his stomach. At least that is how she claims she won my father over."

Helen stared out the window where Mark had climbed out onto the mass of debris to loop a rope around a tangled root mass. Two men in a small rowboat on the river surveyed the mass and called out directions. Mark moved confidently, but it looked like dangerous work. She waited until he was safely back on the bank. "I'm not looking for a way to his heart, only a way to apologize."

"For a plateful of these, I'd forgive you just about anything."

"Even a dog-assisted tumble into a puddle?"

"Ja." Fannie nodded as she licked some of the filling from her fingers. Helen prayed Fannie was right.

"Then I'll set aside a half dozen and brace myself to grovel with them later if I have to."

If she found work with someone before the men came in to eat, she might be spared the pain.

As it turned out, she came up empty while getting to know many of Charlotte's friends and the likable young women of the Bowman family. Clyde had been turned over to some of the children who were wearing him out with a game of fetch. Juliet was occupied with getting a grape from Charlotte, carrying it down to the river to wash and then eat it before racing up the hill to beg for another.

When the men came in, Mark took a seat beside Isaac without so much as a glance in Helen's direction. Before the meal was served, everyone bowed their heads for silent grace. After that, she kept a close eye on the men and noticed Mark took three of her ham and cheese-filled crescent rolls and managed to snag the last of her cream horns when the plate was passed. When he licked a smear of filling from his fingers, she knew he liked them. She'd been smart to keep some back.

She rushed to the house and took the half-dozen pastries outside as she rehearsed her apology. To her chagrin, Mark was already on his way back to the river. She hurried after him and called out, "Mark Bowman, may I speak to you for a moment?"

He stopped and looked back. She saw the indecision cross his face, but he nodded. "I reckon."

Smile. Don't look intimidated.

"I've brought some of my cream horns as a peace offering." She lifted the plate just as her foot encountered Juliet racing past. The outraged raccoon squealed. Helen hopped over her to keep from tripping. Clyde, who until that instant had been fetching a ball for one of the children, leaped on Helen from behind, knocking her forward. She plowed into Mark as he tried to catch her. Horrified, she looked down at the plate of pastry sandwiched between them and then back to his darkening brow. Clyde danced around them, barking excitedly.

"What was it that you wanted?" Mark asked in a cold, calm voice as he held her away. The remains of the smashed cream horns covering his shirt began dropping to the ground. Clyde darted in to snatch them up.

"To apologize," she answered in a small voice. She still had the empty plate in her hands.

"I'm sorry, but I don't know your name. Who are you?"

"I don't think I want to tell you." She began plucking the stuck pieces off his shirt.

He grabbed her hand. "Miss?"

"Zook. Helen Zook. I'm visiting my aunt for the summer, and that's all I'm going to say about it." She turned away and walked back to the tables, aware of the snickers of laughter from the onlookers. She passed them with her head down and went to her aunt.

Charlotte was trying to coax Juliet out of the tree next to the house. Juliet hissed when Helen stopped beside Charlotte and went up to the top of the tree. "Aenti, I'm going to walk home."

"That's a *goot* idea, dear. Poor Juliet is very upset with you."

"I'm afraid she's not the only one." Helen didn't bother looking to see if Mark was still watching her. She could feel his eyes boring into her back.

"I have told Juliet you aren't staying with us long, but I'm not sure she understands me. She isn't fond of company."

"Please tell her I'm sorry I stepped on her." Helen kept walking and didn't look back. She guessed her chance of being hired by Mark Bowman was now about zero or less thanks to Clyde. Things could get desperate if her aunt chose her pet's happiness over her niece and asked Helen to leave.

She wasn't going home, so where would she go?

Paul walked up to Mark, swiped his finger through a clump of cream filling and stuck it in his mouth. "She and that dog together are a menace, but you have to admit she makes a fine dessert."

"Go away."

Paul held out his finger. "Just one more lick?"

"Paul." Mark bit out the name with as much threat as he could manage.

"Okay, okay, I'm going. It's sad to say, because today has been mighty entertaining, but I don't think we will see much of Helen Zook for a while."

"I hope not."

Fannie came down with a wet napkin in her hand. "I thought you might need this."

He took it and began wiping the front of his shirt. "I've never met anyone like that woman."

"I know. Clyde has taken a shine to her and to you. Isn't that *wunderbarr*?"

He looked up in amazement, but Fannie

was already heading back up the hill chuckling to herself.

The rest of the afternoon passed quickly and uneventfully, for which Mark was grateful. The work was hard, but it was satisfying when the jam finally broke free and washed under the bridge. They had gathered enough wood to keep a good many homes warm during the coming winter.

Exhausted and determined not to think about the outspoken and annoying Helen Zook or the troubling letter from Angela, Mark went up to bed not long after supper. With a cool evening breeze blowing through the open window beside him, he fell sound asleep just minutes after his head hit the pillow.

Until the howling began.

Chapter Four

Charlotte entered the kitchen the morning after the frolic and sniffed the air appreciatively. "Something smells *wunderbarr*. What are you making?"

After a sleepless night, Helen had been up mixing, kneading and watching her dough rise for over three hours already, and it was barely seven o'clock. "I'm making chocolate almond crescent rolls."

Because she was unsure if the oven temperature was accurate on her aunt's ancient propane model, she had put only four rolls on her baking sheet to test them first. They were done to a beautiful golden brown. She slid them onto a plate on the table and set the pan aside to cool while she rolled up another dozen. Now if only her decision to see Mark Bowman later today would turn out half so well. She wiped her damp brow with the back of her arm and then rolled up her sleeves.

"May I have one of these?" Charlotte took two from the plate on the kitchen table without waiting for Helen to answer her.

"Help yourself. I'm taking them with me when I go to ask for a job today. I hope Mark Bowman likes them, and I hope he doesn't end up wearing them."

It had occurred to her a little before 3:00 a.m. that it was highly unlikely that today could turn out worse than yesterday, but at least she wouldn't have Clyde or Juliet to hinder her. She planned to go alone to the Bowman workshop.

If Mark would see her, and if she made a sincere effort to apologize, and if she could convince him that she desperately needed a job, he might offer her employment. And if he liked her chocolate almond pastry as much as he had seemed to like her ham and cheese rolls yesterday, she wasn't above using them as a sweetener. It was a lot of ifs, but what choice did she have?

"Why would Mark Bowman want to wear your baked goods?"

Helen drew a deep breath and smiled fondly at her aunt. "I have no idea, but I desperately hope he will offer me a job. He should. I've had experience working in the fabric shop in Nappanee. I worked in a hardware store for a summer, but I didn't care for the man who ran it. He was creepy. I'm conscientious. I'm hardworking. I'm a quick learner. I would be an asset to any business, even one run by a rude, judgmental and annoying fellow like Mark Bowman."

"I don't think he's annoying. Did you let Clyde out this morning?" Charlotte stood in the middle of the kitchen turning in slow circles. She bent down to look under the table then moved the trash can to look behind it as if the dog might have become paper thin overnight.

"I did not."

"He isn't in the house. I've looked everywhere, and Juliet is missing, too." Charlotte opened the door to the cellar and called down the steps, "Clyde, come here, boy."

Helen placed her batch of rolls in the oven, wound the kitchen timer and set it beside the stove. "I'll go outside and look for them in a few minutes. I'm sure they are playing in the yard. You mentioned that Juliet can open a door when she wants to. Was the back door open?"

"I believe it was. I'll look, you finish what you're doing." Charlotte went to the back of the house. She returned a few minutes later. "They aren't outside. I called and called. Clyde never misses a meal, and neither does Juliet. Something is wrong."

"I'm sure they are fine." Helen realized she hadn't heard or seen the dog and raccoon all morning. That was unusual.

Charlotte's eyes widened. She pressed both hands to her cheeks. "Someone has stolen them."

Helen caught herself before she laughed aloud. She struggled to speak in a reasonable tone. "Aenti, calm yourself. Who would want to steal your pets?"

"I've read that the *Englisch* people make hats out of raccoons, and Clyde is a very valuable animal. Why, the bishop's wife remarked on his amazingly long ears just yesterday. Oh, the nerve of that woman to take him from my house. Well, she can't have him. I'm going right over there and tell her so."

Helen caught her aunt by the arm as she marched toward the kitchen door. "*Nee*, you are not going to accuse the bishop's wife of dognapping. She said his ears were foolishly long for such a squat-bodied *hund*. I was standing right beside you when she said it."

"I heard her say his ears were luxuriously long, and she deeply admired such a dog."

Clearly her aunt heard only what she wanted to hear when people were talking about her pets. "Even if she admired him, she wouldn't steal him."

"You don't know that woman. Her family is from Nappanee."

"So is your family."

"Exactly!"

Helen caught the sound of distant barking. "I think I hear him."

"You do?" Charlotte rushed to the door and pulled it open. "Clyde! Where are you?"

Helen moved to stand beside her aunt. Dawn was turning the eastern sky a pale gold color beyond the tree-covered ridge to the east. "I'm sure it was him."

The barking started again, closer now. Charlotte pressed her hands to her chest. "I hear him, too. It is Clyde. Come here, baby boy."

She rushed outside just as a horse and buggy turned off the main road and rolled up her lane. The barking, louder and more frantic now, was coming from the buggy. Helen stepped out onto the porch but almost turned and scurried back into the house when she saw Mark Bowman was driving. What was he doing here? The barking was definitely coming from his buggy. Why did he have Clyde with him?

Mark started to step down, but her aunt planted herself in front of him with one hand on her hip as she shook a finger in his face. "How dare you! I never would have suspected a Bowman of such dastardly behavior."

"What?" He looked utterly confused. Helen knew exactly how he felt.

Charlotte folded her arms over her ample chest. "Stealing is a sin and beneath you, Mark Bowman, but I forgive you, since you have returned him."

Mark looked at Helen. "What is she talking about?"

"She thinks that you stole Clyde."

His puzzled expression snapped into a fierce scowl. "I did no such thing. Your miserable mutt began howling outside my window at three o'clock this morning. I couldn't make him leave. He woke the entire household. I almost returned him then, but I decided to wait until a reasonable hour."

Charlotte already had the rear buggy door open. Clyde was smothering her with doggy kisses as he struggled against the makeshift leash preventing him from jumping out. "Untie him at once, and I won't mention your deplorable behavior to Bishop Beachy."

"I didn't steal your dog!"

Helen patted his shoulder. "I think I can

help. Aenti, listen carefully. Mr. Bowman didn't take Clyde. Your poor dog became lost in the woods last night. Mr. Bowman found him and took time out of his busy morning to bring your precious pet home because he knows how much you love Clyde. Mark is a mighty *goot* fellow."

Charlotte eyed him suspiciously for a long moment and then looked at Helen. Her eyes brightened. "He's a hero just like in the book I'm reading. He rescued poor Clyde from a terrible fate. Bless you, my boy."

"I wouldn't go that far," Mark muttered under his breath. He untied the rope holding Clyde in the buggy.

The overweight hound tumbled out the door and immediately jumped up on Charlotte. She toppled to her backside and hugged him close as he climbed into her lap. "My poor fellow. You are safe at home. *Danki*, Mark. Do come in and join us for breakfast."

"I can't. I must get home." Mark helped Charlotte to her feet.

"Nonsense. I insist. I must reward your efforts on behalf of poor Clyde. My niece makes the most delicious rolls. Where is Juliet?" She rose on tiptoe to try and see the top of his buggy.

"Who is Juliet?" Mark asked, looking to Helen for an explanation.

"Her raccoon."

Charlotte bent to pet her hound. "Juliet is Clyde's dearest friend. They go everywhere together."

"She'll be along shortly," Helen said to appease her aunt.

"Oh, *goot*." She shook a finger at Clyde. "You were a naughty dog to wander off."

Helen leaned toward Mark and whispered, "You haven't seen her, have you?"

He shook his head and leaned closer. "*Nee*. Why are you whispering?"

She jerked her head toward her aunt, who was busy making a fuss over the squirming dog. "I don't want to upset her. She'll start worrying again that someone has made a hat out of her pet."

"Why would she think— *Nee*, never mind. I've been told she's a bit strange. I just didn't realize how strange."

"She's odd, but she's harmless." Odd but oddly endearing, as Helen was learning. She'd never met anyone like her aunt. It was hard to imagine she was related to Helen's stoic father.

"If you say she is harmless, I must believe you." Mark started toward his buggy.

This wasn't how Helen had visualized their meeting, but she wasn't one to let an opportunity slip by. She would ply him with coffee and rolls, apologize and ask him about a job. "Do come inside. I wanted a chance to speak to you about—"

Mark cut her short as he pointed behind her. "I see smoke. Something's burning." He started toward the house.

"My rolls!" Helen dashed around him and up the steps and into the smoke-filled kitchen.

He followed her inside. "Where's your fire extinguisher?"

"I don't know where my aunt keeps it."

"The best time to locate one is before a fire."

"Thanks for the tip." Helen grabbed her hot pads and jerked open the oven door. More smoke billowed into the room. She started coughing, but she managed to pull the pan of charred rolls out and head for the door. He opened the other kitchen window and then followed her outside, coughing and wheezing, too.

Helen plunked the pan on the porch railing and stared at the charred remains through watery eyes. Charlotte came up beside her. "I believe your last batch was better, dear. These look overdone. She'll bring some better ones when she comes to see you later today, Mark."

"See me about what?" he asked.

"Helen desperately wants you to give her

a job. You should. She's conscientious. She's hardworking—"

Helen cut in quickly. "Aenti, he doesn't need to hear this."

"Of course he does. She's a quick learner. She would be an asset to any business, even one run by a rude, judgmental and annoying fellow like you, but I still don't understand why you want to wear her baked goods. That doesn't seem right."

Helen closed her eyes and bowed her head in defeat. She tossed the burned rolls on to the grass. "I was wrong. Today is worse than yesterday." Her voice cracked, but she raised her chin and continued. "I'm so very sorry for your trouble, Mark. Thank you for bringing the dog home. He means a great deal to my *aenti*."

She started into the house. Mark caught her by the arm. "Wait until the smoke clears."

She looked down in surprise at the warmth of his hand on her bare forearm and then looked at his face. She hadn't noticed much about him before except his scowl.

He wasn't a bad-looking fellow. Not as handsome as Joseph, but he had a strong face with a broad forehead, high cheekbones and blond hair that wanted to curl from beneath his hatband. He had a dimple in his left cheek and a small scar in his right eyebrow. His intense green eyes, beneath thick eyelashes, gazed intently at her. They widened slightly, and his pupils darkened as she looked into them. A shiver skittered across her skin.

Mark noticed the smudge of flour on Helen's cheek. The white powder stood in high contrast to the bright blush staining her face. Her gray eyes held specks of blue in their depths, and they glistened with unshed tears of humiliation. She blinked and looked away. Her shoulders slumped. He withdrew his hand and rubbed his tingling palm on the side of his pants. He took a step back. "Find where she keeps the fire extinguisher."

"I will." She sniffed once but didn't look at him.

He took another step back and bumped into the porch railing. "I didn't mean to be rude yesterday."

After a long pause, she nodded slightly. "You had just cause."

He should get going. He didn't understand why he had this urge to linger, except that he didn't want to see her cry. "My brother and my cousin say that I can be overbearing. If I was, I'm sorry."

"I don't know what's the matter with me.

Why can't a single thing go right? Everything used to be so easy." She covered her face with her hands, and her shoulders started shaking.

He stepped closer. "Please don't cry over a few burned rolls."

She made a sound like a strangled sob and fled around the corner of the house, leaving him feeling foolish and brutish at the same time. Every time he tried to help, he seemed to make things worse. She managed to fluster him, and he didn't like the feeling. He turned to her aunt. "Will she be okay?"

"*Ja*, we have plenty of flour."

"Flour?" He didn't follow her.

"To make more rolls for you so that you will give her a job." Charlotte smiled sweetly.

"I don't need a baker. I need an inventory clerk and a general office worker. Has she had any experience?"

Charlotte held her hands up and raised her eyes to the sky. "I shudder to tell you the experiences that child has had. I'm amazed at how well she is handling it."

"Handling what? Never mind. I need to get going. Tell Helen to come by the shop tomorrow, and I will interview her for the job, but I can't promise anything." He didn't want to know more about Helen, and he didn't want to try and stay in a conversation with Charlotte Zook. It was an impossibility.

"All right. Do send Juliet home directly when you see her."

"Juliet? Oh, the raccoon. Sure." He nodded and made his escape.

As he turned his horse and buggy toward home, he glanced over his shoulder, but Helen remained out of sight. He felt a stab of pity for her. Living with Charlotte Zook couldn't be easy. The woman was odd to say the least. He might pity Helen, but he wouldn't hire her unless she was right for the job. So far, he hadn't seen anything that suggested she would be.

It had been a mistake to tell the aunt he'd discuss a job with Helen. He'd spoken in a moment of weakness, and that wasn't like him. Something about Helen left him feeling off-kilter.

Besides which, her assessment of his character continued to go downhill. He'd gone from being rude and judgmental to annoying, as well. He was confident Charlotte had been repeating what Helen had said about him.

He chuckled as he recalled the look of horror on Helen's face when her aunt started listing her qualifications. She knew what was coming. It served her right for her less-than-charitable comments about him. A man looking for a humble, modest and mild-mannered wife wouldn't find those qualities in Helen Zook.

Leaning back in the buggy seat, his smile faded as he imagined interviewing her. He'd already interviewed a half dozen people for the job, and none of them had been right. His brother said he was too picky, but his uncle's business was important, and hiring the wrong person was worse than working shorthanded.

Mark glanced back at Charlotte's house. Unless he was sadly mistaken, Helen wouldn't be right for the position either, but he would do her the courtesy of giving her a chance. If she showed up. From the way she had rushed off in tears, he didn't imagine she would find the courage to face him again anytime soon.

Chapter Five

Helen came out of her room a few minutes after she heard the buggy drive away. She stopped in the bathroom to splash cold water on her face and erase the marks of her tears. The burn of humiliation would linger much longer. How would she ever face Mark again?

She stared at her pale face in the mirror. Perhaps this was part of God's plan to make her a humbler person. If that was the case, it was working.

She had always taken pride in her accomplishments and in her intelligence, although she knew they were gifts from God. She'd been the brightest scholar in school. *Englisch* customers in the fabric shop often commented on how friendly she was. Many of the young men she walked out with before settling on Joseph had said she was the prettiest young woman in her community. Prettier and smarter than her sister.

Helen was the better cook, the better quilter, the better seamstress. Olivia never truly excelled at anything. More than once, Helen had heard her referred to as the simple sister in the Zook family. Olivia wasn't simple. Things just didn't come easily for her.

Helen sighed. There had been pride in her heart because of Joseph, too. He had been the most sought-after and eligible bachelor in their community. She had set her sights on winning him even after she knew her sister was in love with him. When he asked for Helen's hand in marriage she had been overjoyed, but look how that triumph had turned out for her. She became a laughingstock when Joseph broke their engagement to marry the "simple" sister.

No doubt this morning's adventure along with yesterday's disaster would be recounted to the entire Bowman clan and beyond for many more laughs at her expense. She wouldn't be able to look anyone in the eye. Her summer would be spent living off the charity of her aunt and avoiding the community as much as possible. And then what? When the summer was over, where did she go? Home? She couldn't go there. Was she destined to travel to yet another distant place and start over somewhere new?

She turned away from her reflection. Despair wasn't an expression she wore well.

Her aunt was seated at the table with a cup of coffee in front of her when Helen entered the kitchen. The room was clear of smoke, but the smell of burned bread lingered. Clyde lay on the floor beside her aunt's feet. He looked sadder than usual, with his heavy jowls spread over his front feet and his eyes half-closed.

"He hasn't touched his food," Charlotte said, staring down at him.

"Perhaps Mr. Bowman fed him before he brought him here."

"I expect you're right. That Mark is a mighty nice fella. It's a shame he has a girlfriend back home. Clyde and I think he'd make an excellent match for you."

"*Nee*, he would not. I can't abide men with green eyes." Or one with a dimple in his left cheek, thick dark eyelashes and a sour expression whenever he looked at her. Helen crossed to the oven and turned it off.

"Have you decided not to make more rolls?"

"There isn't much sense in wasting more of my time and your supplies." Helen began cleaning up.

"I guess that's true. You don't need to tempt

Mark with sweets since he has given you the job."

Helen spun around. "What did you say?"

"You don't have to tempt him with sweets, although I'm sure he would enjoy them."

"He told you he is willing to hire me?"

"*Ja*, something like that."

Helen sat down opposite her aunt and took her by the hand. "Tell me exactly what he said, Aenti. This is important."

"Exactly?"

"Word for word."

Charlotte closed her eyes. "Let me think. I believe he said he didn't need a baker, but he did need an inventory clerk and a general office worker. I'm sure that's what he told me. Clyde certainly has taken a liking to him. I have, too."

"But what did he say about *me*?"

"He said to tell you to come by the shop later today and start work. He couldn't promise that you would like the job, but he did promise to tell Juliet to come home as soon as he saw her."

Helen was almost afraid to hope. Could it be true? "He is giving me a job? Aenti, are you sure that's what he said?"

Charlotte smiled and gave Helen's hand a quick squeeze. "People often accuse me of not listening, but I hear well enough. Sometimes I even hear what isn't said. You want a job. Mark needs help."

She patted Helen's hand, took a drink of coffee, rose and carried the mug to the sink. "You must hurry if you are going to get another batch of crescent rolls done and get to work on time. You should take my bicycle. It will be faster than walking."

"He actually said I had the job?" Helen's spirits rose like a kite in a strong wind.

"Honestly, Helen, I'm beginning to think you are the one who doesn't listen. I'm sure your sister and your fiancé told you many times that they were falling in love with each other even though they struggled against it."

Helen's bright mood plummeted. "*Nee*, they never mentioned it. They went behind my back and met in secret."

"I thought Olivia was working for Joseph's mother? They would have had a reason to see each other every day. I'm sure I read that in one of your mother's letters. I keep all my correspondence in boxes. I can look for it."

"Joseph's mother had to have surgery, and Olivia went to help with the housework and nurse her for a few weeks. I couldn't do it. I had to help Mamm get ready for the wedding."

"Olivia has always had a sweet and caring nature. I'm sure she was glad to help."

"She helped herself to my fiancé," Helen said bitterly. "I don't want to talk about it."

"Pain is part of life, but it's hard to heal in silence. Talking helps. I shall pray for your sister. I'm sure she has been hurt by your actions."

"My actions? What did I do?"

"You turned your back on her and cut her out of your life just when she most needed your forgiveness. Well, it can't be changed. Water under the bridge as they say. I've always wondered who *they* are, but I guess I'm one of *them*, for I just said it. The Lord has a plan for us all, Helen. Including you. Now I must go look for Juliet. What time will you be home from work?"

"I'm not sure." Grateful that her aunt had changed the subject, Helen turned the oven back on. After her aunt had gone out, Helen started on a new batch of rolls. She was determined not to think about Olivia and Joseph, but it was impossible in the quiet house with only the ticking of the timer to fill the silence.

Joseph had tried to tell her about his growing feelings for Olivia. Helen had refused to listen. She knew she could make him forget her sister in time. None of that excused his betrayal. It might be water under the bridge because their marriage couldn't be undone, but she wasn't ready to forgive him or her sister.

Strangely, her anger toward them didn't burn as brightly as it once had. It was giving way to sorrow. She missed her sister and her parents.

An hour later, with a basket of still-warm rolls in an insulated bag over her arm, Helen rode her aunt's bike the two miles to Bowmans Crossing and entered the front door of the workshop a few minutes before nine. The large room was already bustling with activity as a half-dozen men operated various machines. The smell of wood shavings, diesel fumes and the loud hum of engines filled the air.

Off to her right, she noticed an interior window into what appeared to be an office. A young dark-haired woman dressed in jeans and a bright yellow and red print blouse sat at a desk. Helen stepped inside, and the noise dropped away when she closed the door behind her. The woman looked up from a computer and smiled. "Welcome to Bowman's Amish Furniture. I'm Jessica Clay. How may I help you?"

"I'm Helen Zook. Mark Bowman is expecting me."

Her eyebrows shot up. "He is? He didn't mention he had a client appointment."

"I'm not a customer. I'm here to start a new job. Inventory clerk and general office worker. I'm guessing that means I'll be working in here with you."

Jessica's smile widened. "Awesome. I could sure use the help. Mark's gone to arrange for a special order of hardware from John Miller, the local blacksmith. He should be back in an hour or so."

Helen sat on the edge of a small upholstered bench and tried to still her racing heart as she clutched her basket. Jessica seemed pleasant enough. The office was small but neat, with a wide exterior window that let in the sunshine as well as the interior one that overlooked the work area. She was surprised to see a number of modern devices. "The local bishop must be very progressive to allow phones, a fax machine and a computer in an Amish business."

"We get questions about it all the time from our customers who are familiar with Amish ways. Isaac Bowman has a silent partner named James Carter. He's a furniture dealer in Cincinnati, and he isn't Amish. James had the computer and phone installed and even had a website built for the business. We now have satellite phone and internet. It was actually Mark who suggested it as a way to make the business more productive."

"But I didn't see any electric lines to the building."

"The business is powered by a diesel generator, in keeping with the rules of Isaac's church. Because of that, we are able to have a limited amount of technology, which I run since I'm not Amish, either. The Bowmans do have permission to have a phone in here so they don't have to use the phone shack up the road that the other Amish families use. We also have a few solar panels for charging cell phones and pagers for the volunteer firemen who work here."

"I have heard of Amish churches who are this progressive but I've never met anyone from such a church." She wondered what other rules were different from the ones her congregation had.

Jessica returned to her computer but soon said, "Something smells delish."

Helen smiled and placed the basket on the corner of the desk. "I've brought some treats as a thank-you for Mark, but help yourself. I made plenty."

Jessica moved her chair closer. "Are you sure?"

"Absolutely." Folding back the red-and-white napkin, Helen unfastened the insulated bag and offered the basket to her.

The door opened, and a tall blond Amish man leaned in. "Jessica, has Mr. Barker decided if he wants six or eight chairs with his dining set, because I'll have to special order more walnut if he wants eight."

"Let me check our email again, but I don't think so. Samuel, this is Helen Zook. Mark hired her."

"He did? He never mentioned it to me." He stepped inside and closed the door.

"It was only this morning," Helen said.

His surprise was apparent. "This morning? Mark hired you this morning? Wait. Zook? Are you the one with the dog?"

Helen wished everyone didn't look so shocked by the news that Mark had hired her. Why hadn't he told anyone? "My aunt owns the dog. I'm sorry if he disrupted your sleep."

"He sure enough did that. I'm Samuel Bowman. My father Isaac owns this business. Didn't I see you at the frolic?"

"I was there for a little while." Helen clenched her lips together. The less said about that day the better.

"These rolls are amazing." Jessica licked her fingers. "Try one, Samuel."

"Please do," Helen said quickly offering him the basket.

"Danki." Samuel took one. "The email, Jessica?"

"Right." She spun back to the computer and started typing. "He did reply. Says here he only wants six. Problem solved."

"These are *wunderbarr*," Samuel said taking another bite. "I don't suppose you brought enough to share with everyone. I feel a little guilty enjoying this while the men working out there get nothing."

"I made three dozen. There's plenty to go around. Is there *kaffee*?"

"In the break room," Jessica said. "I'll go make some. Cream or sugar?"

"Just black." Helen quickly folded a half-dozen rolls in the napkin and then handed the basket to Jessica. "Take these with you so the men can enjoy them on their break."

Jessica went out the door. No sooner had it closed behind her than the phone started ringing. Samuel smiled and nodded toward it. "Might as well get started."

"Me? Oh, *ja*, I reckon so." Helen went to the desk and picked up the phone. "Bowman's Amish Furniture, this is Helen Zook. How may I help you?"

She quickly wrote down the customer's

order and his contact information as Samuel stood at the counter listening to her end of the conversation. When she hung up, she handed him her notes. "Mr. Fielding in Akron wishes to order three bedroom suites for his furniture showroom. He has sold the ones he purchased before. He says you'll know which styles he wants. Is there anything else I should have asked him?"

"*Nee*, this looks great. He didn't by chance say he needed a custom fireplace mantel, did he?"

"He didn't. Should I have asked that?"

Samuel gave her a wry smile and shook his head. "We had a customer cancel his order for one after Mark finished carving it. Since Mark isn't here, why don't I give you a quick tour. We have our main workroom out there where you came in. The break room is the next door down."

Helen followed him as he crossed the office to a door opposite the one she had entered. "Through here is our showroom. We keep a few dozen pieces on display and for sale, but most of our work is shipped to furniture stores in different parts of the country."

In a large room, well lit by numerous sky-lights overhead, Helen saw dining tables and chairs, bedroom sets, armoires, benches, side tables and even butcher-block islands. She admired the workmanship in the solid wood pieces. One in particular caught her eye. A beam almost six feet long sat on a pair of saw-horses. A forest scene with cavorting foxes in carved relief covered the entire length. "Is that the mantel you were talking about?"

"It is. It's still raw wood. Mark hasn't chosen a finish for it yet. Foxes aren't as popular as wolves or deer, but I'm hopeful we can sell it." He glanced at the memo she had taken. "I'll check if we have any of these in stock. I think we do."

"Should I wait for Mark to give me my instructions?"

"I'm sure Jessica can keep you busy until Mark returns. Have her tell the fellas to take an early break and enjoy those rolls. And tell her to save one more for me." He walked to the far end of the room.

Helen returned to the office to find Isaac Bowman conferring with Jessica over a ledger. Outside, a pickup pulling a horse trailer turned into the parking lot and stopped. A middle-aged couple in riding clothes got out and came inside. Isaac left Jessica's side to welcome them. "How may we help you?"

The man held out his hand. "I'm Vern Jenks, and this is my wife, Theresa. We've just come from the Stroud Stables where we mentioned we were looking for some authentic Amish-made furniture, and Connie Stroud suggested we stop in here."

Isaac nodded. "Noah, my youngest *sohn*, works for Connie. She is a *goot* neighbor."

"And a fine horse trainer," Theresa added. "We've just picked up a new hunter for our daughter."

"What type of furniture are you looking for?" Isaac asked.

"Rustic," Theresa said. "Reclaimed barn wood, unusual pieces. I'm redoing our hunt club meeting room in American primitive."

Isaac pulled on his long gray beard. "I don't believe we have what you are looking for, but we do custom work. If you can give us an idea of what you want, we can make it for you."

Theresa's expression fell. "I'm not sure I want to wait for custom pieces to be built. If I change my mind, I'll let you know."

Helen could tell the couple wouldn't be back, but she couldn't let them walk away without at least trying to make a sale. "Is there a fireplace in the room you are redecorating?"

Theresa nodded. "There is."

"Then there is something you might like in our showroom. It's a hand-carved primitive fireplace mantel that would go beautifully in a hunt club setting. The wood is unfinished and could be stained or painted, if you like, or left raw under a clear-coat finish."

Isaac grinned. "I'd forgotten about Mark's piece. Right this way, folks. *Danki*, Helen."

Jessica clapped softly when the door closed behind them. "Nice going, newbie. Let's hope they buy it. Now I have some filing for you to do."

Helen smiled and breathed a sigh of relief. She was going to enjoy working with these people.

Mark entered the front door of the workshop and stopped in his tracks. Where was everyone? The machines were all sitting idle. He glanced into the office. It was empty except for an Amish woman in a blue dress and black apron standing behind the desk at the file cabinet. She had her back to him, but he knew it had to be the wife of one of his cousins. They sometimes came to help out.

He opened the office door and stepped in. "Where is everyone?"

She squeaked and spun around. It was Helen.

So she did have enough pluck to face him again. He was surprised and a little pleased, but he couldn't let that show. He scowled at her. "What are you doing?"

"Filing."

"Filing what?"

"Paid invoices. Jessica asked me to do it."

"Where is Jessica? Where is everyone?"

"In the break room."

He glanced at the clock on the wall. "It's not break time."

"I'm afraid I'm to blame. I brought some rolls, and everyone seems to like them. Isaac and Samuel thought the men might enjoy them while they were still warm. I saved some for you."

She picked up a red-and-white checkered napkin bundle and held it toward him. "I'm so very grateful for this job. You won't regret hiring me. I won't disappoint you."

He tilted his head to the side. "When did I hire you?"

"What do you mean?"

"It's a pretty simple question. When did I hire you? *Nee*, let me rephrase that. I haven't hired you. I haven't even interviewed you."

She pulled her arms to her chest and clutched the bundle tightly in both hands. "But Aenti Charlotte said you wanted me to start work today."

"Well, Aenti Charlotte got it wrong. I'll

hazard a guess that's not the first time that has happened."

The office door opened. Mark turned to see Jessica and Samuel enter. They were both grinning. Samuel clapped a hand on Mark's shoulder. "Mark, you picked a winner. The men love your crescent rolls, Helen."

Jessica took her seat. "Not only does Helen have typing skills and a pleasant phone voice, and she knows how to file, but she also knows how to use the fax machine. I'm impressed with your choice, Mark."

"I learned to use a fax machine at my last job, but that was before I was baptized. I'm not sure how your bishop would feel about me using it now unless it was an emergency."

Helen pushed a slip of paper across the desk. "Jessica, here are your phone messages. The receipts are filed and Samuel, Mr. Barker says Mrs. Barker has changed her mind and wants eight chairs. I took the liberty of calling several local lumberyards. The one in Berlin says they have the type of walnut you're looking for.

"*Goot.* Order it. I'll have Luke pick it up tomorrow."

"I will," she said as Samuel went out and closed the door behind him.

"*Nee*, you will not," Mark said. "You are not an employee here."

"She acts like an employee to me," Jessica said. "Besides, I'm tired of doing the work of two people because you can't make up your mind and hire someone."

"Hiring the right worker takes thoughtful consideration. I won't be rushed into a decision."

"Well, you'd better hurry, or you'll be giving thoughtful consideration to hiring two people instead of one. I can get a job anywhere. I happen to like working here because it is close to home and Isaac is so very sweet, but I'm not married to this job."

Helen stepped up beside Jessica. "Please, don't quarrel because of me. My aunt misunderstood. She's a little eccentric, and she got it wrong."

Helen lowered her eyes and clasped her hands together in front of her, wringing the napkin into a tight ball. "If you would grant me an interview, I would be deeply grateful."

He gave a dismissive wave of his hand. "I don't see you working out. I'm sorry."

Jessica folded her arms across her chest and gave him a sour glare. "You should reconsider."

"I'm not going to change my mind. She isn't right for the job."

The outside door opened again, and Isaac leaned in. "Helen, we're happy to have you with us. I would have let a sale walk right out the door today if not for your quick thinking. She sold your mantel, Mark. You made a *goot* choice when you hired her. I was beginning to worry about your ability to know the right kind of worker when you met one. I'm pleased my faith in you wasn't misplaced."

Mark swallowed the denial that rose to his lips. How could he argue with his uncle? This was his business after all. "*Danki,* Onkel."

Isaac closed the door, and Jessica burst out laughing. "I can't wait to hear you tell him why you fired her."

Mark pressed his lips together. "I can't fire someone I haven't hired."

Helen took a step closer. "I will go explain to Isaac what has happened."

He shook his head. "Never mind. Come with me. I'll show you where we store our inventory and go over our ordering practices."

She squealed and grinned, her pretty gray eyes sparkling with happiness. "*Danki.* I'll do my best for the company. I'll work hard every day. You won't be sorry."

He already was. "This is a trial period only. One month. Your work will have to speak for itself."

"I won't let you down. Here, these are for you." She forced a smile and handed him the napkin. He unwound it. Inside was a pile of chocolate-covered pieces of bread.

She pressed a hand to her lips. "Oh, I guess they got a little squished, but they should still taste fine."

"I'm not hungry. I'm worried."

"About what?"

He handed the napkin back to her. "About the next disaster you'll bring down on our heads."

Chapter Six

Helen quietly followed Mark as he detailed the jobs he expected her to do. She'd had the forethought to bring a small notebook and pencil, so she was able to take notes as he went along.

He pushed open the swinging door of a room off the main woodworking shop. "This is where we keep most of our non-lumber supplies."

Helen saw three sides of the room were lined floor to ceiling with bins in different sizes, all neatly labeled. The other side of the room held a large pegboard where various types of tools hung, also neatly labeled.

"You will need to keep an accurate inventory of parts, tools and hardware. Notify me when any items are running low. Each bin has the name of the item on the front and the minimal count number. For instance, this is our most popular cabinet pull." He opened one of the drawers. "The lowest the count should ever be is sixteen."

"Will I order more or simply notify you?"

"Notify me to start with. After you've been here awhile, I may let you take over ordering. If you make it past your probation."

"What type of inventory counting system do you use? A computer program or ledger?"

He eyed her closely. "Ledger."

"How often will I do cycle counts?" She scribbled a note to herself.

"Weekly on Mondays. You've done this before, haven't you?"

"I worked in a small fabric shop for several years. Our inventory was fabric, buttons and threads, not hardware and wood. We did monthly cycle counts." Helen saw the beginnings of respect in his eyes. She could handle this job, and she would prove it.

He slipped his thumbs under his suspenders. "A lot of inventory issues stem from improper employee training."

She nodded. "I agree. Inventory inaccuracy, damage and misidentification can usually be traced to mistakes made by people."

He frowned slightly. "As I was saying,

proper training increases a business's efficiency and cuts down on inventory issues."

She resisted the urge to laugh at his pompous demeanor. Instead, she clasped the notebook in front of her and tried to appear the eager pupil. "I look forward to learning all I can from you. May I see the ledger so I can familiarize myself with your inventory?"

"It's on my desk."

She looked around. "Will I be working in here or will I be in the office?"

"Where would you like to work?"

"Out front with Jessica to begin with. I know I'll have a lot of questions, and it will save running back and forth if I'm out there where I can ask someone without interrupting you needlessly."

"I'll have a desk put up front for you."

"Who are your main suppliers? We should send them a card or letter letting them know I'll be placing orders when my training is over."

"Your concern should be making it past the thirty-day mark." He turned on his heels and left the room.

Helen took a deep breath and sent up a quick prayer that she could do just that.

She made it through the rest of the day without subjecting Mark to a new disaster, in spite of his concerns. When he left to meet with one of their local wood suppliers, Helen was handed over to Samuel and Jessica. Her head was spinning with all the information poured over her in a single day, but she took copious notes and remained convinced that she could do the job.

When she arrived home just after five o'clock, she found her aunt pacing in the kitchen, distraught with worry. Her shoes were muddy. Her dress was torn at the hem, and her *kapp* was missing. Juliet hadn't come home.

"I don't know where she can be. I've called and I've called. I have searched everywhere." Charlotte paced the floor of the kitchen, returning again and again to look out the door.

Helen hadn't spared a thought the entire day for her aunt or her aunt's missing pet, and her conscience smote her. She slipped her arm over her aunt's shoulders. "I'm so sorry. I'll help you look for her."

"Will you? Bless you, dear."

"Sit down for a few minutes and catch your breath. Let's think about where she might have gone. Have you had anything to eat today?"

"Not since breakfast. I'm just so worried."

Helen steered her aunt to the table. "Sit and I'll make you a cup of coffee. When you've had a bit of a rest, we can put our heads together and figure out what to do next."

As the coffee perked, Helen fixed a couple of chicken salad sandwiches from leftovers in her aunt's propane-powered refrigerator. She set a plate in front of Charlotte. Taking a seat, Helen folded her hands and said a silent prayer of grace. When she was finished, she took a bite of her sandwich.

Charlotte glanced over her shoulder toward the door, where Clyde lay on his rug with his head on his paws and his eyes fixed on Juliet's empty bed. His food remained untouched in his bowl. "He's so sad. I worry about him."

"Aenti, has Juliet ever disappeared like this before?"

"Only once. She was gone for an entire day but not overnight. That was weeks ago. She's been content to be with us ever since."

"That should make you feel better to know she came back once before."

"I reckon it should, but it doesn't." Charlotte's tone was so dejected that Helen's heart went out to her.

Helen got up to pour them both a cup of freshly brewed coffee. "Do you know where she was when she stayed away before?"

"I saw her follow another raccoon into the forest."

"Another raccoon? So perhaps she has a friend she has gone to visit. That seems the most likely possibility."

Charlotte pushed her half-eaten sandwich aside. "You don't think some terrible person made her into a hat, do you?"

"I do not. She wears a pretty pink collar. That would tell anyone she's a pet." But it wouldn't prevent Juliet from returning to the wild if the instinct was strong enough.

"She could be caught in a trap."

Helen shook her head vigorously. "It's not trapping season. That takes place in the winter. Please try not to worry. Finish your sandwich, and we'll go look for her together."

"You must think I'm a *narrish* old woman to go on so about a raccoon."

"I don't think you're crazy."

"I raised her from a baby. Clyde found her in the forest and brought her home to me. He seemed to know she needed help. They've been devoted to each other ever since and to me. Clyde and Juliet don't care that I'm absentminded. They don't mind that I talk to myself or that I'm different. They don't make fun of me behind my back as some of the children do. They just love me. They are kinder than many people."

Helen reached across the table to lay her

hand on Charlotte's forearm. "Your family loves you, Aenti Charlotte."

"I know, but they are far away, and letters can't give me a hug when I'm lonely. Listen to me prattle. I'm sorry, Helen, I haven't even asked about your new job today. How was it? Did you enjoy it?"

Helen shook a finger in mock annoyance. "I have a bone to pick with you about that."

Charlotte folded her hands as her gaze shifted from Helen to the ceiling. "With me? Whatever for?"

"Mark Bowman didn't tell you he wanted to hire me."

Charlotte sighed and reached for the sugar bowl. "He didn't?"

"He did not."

After spooning two lumps of sugar into her cup, Charlotte stirred it slowly. "Did I get that mixed up? Well, it doesn't matter. You were hired, weren't you? I knew you'd do an excellent job, and I'm sure Mark quickly saw what an asset you are."

"I'm not sure he would call me an asset yet, but I did get the job." Although not because Mark wanted her to have it.

"And you like it?"

"It's okay. I have a lot to learn. It's not

permanent yet. I was hired on a thirty-day trial basis."

Charlotte raised her cup to her lips and peeked at Helen from beneath her lashes. "And you like Mark?"

Helen drew back. "I most certainly do not like him."

"Oh. I thought you might have changed your mind. He does have nice eyes."

"But he has terrible manners." Helen opened her mouth to list his flaws but quickly changed her mind. It wouldn't do to have her aunt repeating her comments, even if they were true. Helen suspected Mark would welcome an excuse to fire her.

"Did he enjoy the crescent rolls you baked for him?"

Helen chuckled. "He never got to try them, but at least he didn't end up wearing them."

"Will you bake something again tomorrow for him?"

Helen turned the idea over in her mind. She enjoyed baking more than just about anything. "I think so. The people at the business gobbled up what I took in today. I think I'll make cinnamon rolls."

"That sounds *wunderbarr*. With raisins and icing?"

"Is that the way you like them?"

"*Ja.* Lots of icing."

"Then that's what I'll make, and I'll leave plenty here for you."

"*Danki.* Can we go look for Juliet now?"

"Of course. Did you take Clyde with you when you searched earlier?"

"I did."

If Clyde with his keen nose couldn't locate Juliet, Helen doubted they would be able to find her, but she didn't voice her thoughts.

It was fully dark when they returned to the house, having searched up and down the river and woods in both directions without success. Clyde had cast about continually for a scent, but Helen had no idea if he was searching for his friend or a rabbit to chase.

Helen closed the door and lit the lamp over the kitchen table. "If she doesn't come by morning, we'll ask the neighbors to help us look for her."

"Whatever am I to do if I don't find her?" Charlotte wailed. She covered her face with her hands and sobbed.

Helen gathered her weeping aunt into her arms. "Don't give up. It's only been a day. I'm sure she'll come home tonight. If she doesn't, tomorrow we'll spread the word that she is missing. I'll tell the Bowmans and the people at the workshop. Someone may have seen her and not realized we are looking for her. The more eyes we have helping us the better."

"You are so practical, Helen. You know just what to do."

After helping her exhausted aunt to bed a half hour later, Helen turned on the battery-powered night-light that sat on Charlotte's dresser. Clyde was curled in his dog bed in the corner, snoring loudly. Helen started out the door but stopped when her aunt spoke.

"I wasn't happy when you first arrived and told me you were staying for the summer," Charlotte said in a small voice. "I like living alone, but now I'm very glad you are with me."

"I'm glad that I'm here, too," Helen said quietly and closed the door.

In her room, Helen unpinned her *kapp* and hung it from a peg on the wall. She let her hair down and rubbed the top of her scalp where it sometimes got tender by the end of the day. After donning her nightgown, she sat on the edge of the bed and started brushing her hip-length hair.

So much had happened, it was hard to believe it had only been one day since the frolic. Like a child on a teeter-totter, she had gone from the low of her early-morning baking calamity to the high of getting a job and proving her worth to her new employer.

She chuckled as she remembered the look on Mark's face when Isaac praised her and complimented Mark for hiring her. Clearly, his uncle's approval meant more to him than getting rid of her, otherwise she would have been out the door in short order. Would she be able to earn Mark's respect and keep her job? It surprised her how much she wanted to do so. He'd seen her at her worst. She wanted him to see her at her best. It'd be good to have him look at her without disgust or anger in his eyes. His "pretty green eyes," as her aunt was fond of saying. He did have nice eyes, and he might have a sweet smile if he used it once in a while.

The high point of her day had given way to a new low again upon seeing her aunt's anguish over her missing pet this evening. Helen was deeply touched by Charlotte's admission that she was glad to have her here at such a time. She'd never thought much about her father's odd sister except to wonder why she hadn't married. To Helen that had seemed like a fate worse than death and yet, by her own admission, Charlotte was happy living alone. Perhaps that was true, but people needed people to care about them.

Helen finished brushing her hair. As she braided it, her thoughts turned back to Mark. What would he have to say to her tomorrow? Hopefully, he'd find some time to enjoy one of her cinnamon rolls and their day would get off to a better start. It was hard to imagine getting off to a worse one. Still, her morning's difficulties had ended in a job, so it wasn't a total loss.

She had never had to work so hard for something in her life.

Now, if only Juliet would see fit to come home tonight and take one worry off her shoulders.

Helen tied a ribbon to the end of her braid and knelt to say her prayers. It suddenly occurred to her she hadn't thought about Joseph once since early that morning.

Mark sat bolt upright in bed as the hound's baying reverberated through his open window. "Not again!"

A glance at the clock on his wall showed it was four thirty. He jumped out of bed and headed to the window. He could just make out Clyde's white face pointing to the sky at the base of the tree through the foliage below. "Go home, you foolish dog!"

Clyde rose on his back feet, planted his

front feet on the tree trunk and howled louder. The whole house would be awake in no time. Mark thrust his feet in his slippers, pulled a robe over his pajamas and rushed toward the stairs. His uncle looked out from his bedroom door as Mark went past. "I'll take care of him, Onkel."

"Why doesn't she keep him at home?"

"I don't know, but I'm going to make certain Helen understands this isn't acceptable."

"It's Charlotte's dog, not Helen's." Isaac closed the bedroom door, and Mark went downstairs. It might not be Helen's dog, but she was going to have to control him if Charlotte wouldn't.

Mark opened the back door. In the moonlight, he saw Clyde was still standing with his front paws on the tree trunk, gazing upward. Another mournful howl rent the air. Mark grabbed him by his collar and pulled him away from the tree.

"Enough. Go home. Get." He pointed toward the bridge.

Clyde wagged his tail happily and woofed, but he didn't get.

"Come on. It's this way," Mark clapped his hands and walked a few feet toward the road. *"Goot hund."*

The dog darted back to the tree, stood on his hind legs and howled a long, lonesome cry.

Mark jumped to grab his collar again. "Bad dog. You are going home, and this time I'm not waiting until a decent hour to return you. We'll find out if Helen and Charlotte like being rousted out of bed in the middle of the night."

He turned around to see Paul standing in the open doorway without his usual grin. He rubbed his face with both hands and headed toward the barn. "I'll go hitch up the buggy and take him back this time."

"Hitch the buggy, but I'll take him." Mark couldn't wait to see Helen and tell her exactly what he thought of her crazy mutt.

The dog climbed in the buggy willingly and scrambled onto the front seat when Paul opened the door for him. "He looks eager to go home."

"I wish he would stay home." Having dressed for the day, because he knew he wouldn't be getting any more sleep, Mark climbed in and picked up the reins. Clyde tried to crawl into Mark's lap. He pushed the dog away, muttering under his breath.

"What was that?" Paul asked, a grin pulling at one side of his mouth.

"If you still want to drive him home, you can because I have better things to do."

Paul held up both hands. "*Nee*, he chose to serenade your window. I think he likes you."

Clyde licked Mark's ear and woofed. Paul burst out laughing. "See. He does like you. Shall I open the shop for you?"

Mark wiped the side of his head with his shirt sleeve. "I'll be back to do that. Just make sure the generator is fueled."

"I will, *bruder*. Enjoy your buggy ride."

Mark clicked his tongue to get the horse moving. As they pulled away from the house, Clyde hung his head out the window and howled a long, lonely note. Once they passed through the covered bridge, the dog lay down on the seat with his head on his paws.

When Mark turned in Helen's lane, he saw light pouring out the kitchen windows. Someone was already up. So much for his intention to rouse Helen from a sound sleep to see how she liked it. He pulled his horse to a stop at the hitching rail and got out. The dog tumbled out after him and waddled to the front porch. Mark followed.

Through the window, he saw Helen, wearing a dark blue dress and a black apron, standing at the kitchen table with her back to him. Her hair hung down in a long blond braid the color of ripe wheat in the sun. Instead of a prayer *kapp*, she wore a white kerchief tied at the nape of her neck. She was humming as she mixed something in a large bowl. The movement sent her braid swinging back and forth. He wondered what it would look like unbound. In his mind he could see it spread out like a cape of golden ripples shimmering in the light.

He shook off the fanciful thought and knocked on the door. She spun around, her eyes wide. She had another smudge of flour on her face, this time above her left eyebrow. He opened the door and stepped inside. Clyde squeezed past him and rushed to her, dancing about her legs with his tongue lolling and his tail wagging so fast it was almost a blur.

Her astonished gaze went from Mark's face to the dog and back again. He folded his arms over his chest and glared at her.

Chapter Seven

The wonderful smell of baking bread filled the kitchen, making it hard for Mark to maintain his ire. He'd barely eaten any supper last night, and he hadn't had breakfast.

Helen's look of astonishment changed to one of defeat. "Not again."

"My words exactly when he woke me from a sound sleep. Again."

The dog ambled to his dish and began eating.

Helen met Mark's gaze, her eyes filled with remorse. "I am so sorry. I thought he was still in my aunt's bedroom. I wonder how he got out."

"I don't know, but could you make sure it doesn't happen again?"

"I'll certainly try." She glanced toward the doorway into the living room and lowered her voice. "At least you brought him home before Aenti Charlotte woke up. I thank you for that. She was so upset last night over Juliet's disappearance that I was worried about her."

He heard the genuine concern in her voice, and his conscience stabbed him. His intention hadn't been to do something kind. Just the opposite. "Her raccoon hasn't returned?"

Helen shook her head. "*Nee*, she hasn't yet. Aenti Charlotte is beside herself."

"Is that unusual?" he asked, letting his sarcasm slip out.

She pinned him with a pointed look. "My aunt may be a trifle odd, but she loves her pets. They are like her family."

Looking down, he shifted his weight from one foot to the other. He deserved the rebuke in her tone. Few Amish looked upon dogs as anything but working animals to guard the farms or herd livestock, but he had no right to judge Charlotte Zook harshly because she felt differently. "The raccoon might not come back. She's a wild animal for all your aunt treats her like a child."

"That was my thought, too." A ringing sound came from behind Helen. She spun around, sending her braid flying out like a rope as it swung over her shoulder. She picked up a kitchen timer and turned it off, then donned a pair of oven mitts and pulled a tray of cinnamon buns from the oven. They smelled and looked wonderful. His stomach growled loudly.

She shot a quick smile his way. "You're welcome to one of these as soon as I frost them. Would you like some coffee? It should be ready." She set the pan on a wire rack to cool and flipped her braid back over her shoulder with a careless gesture that was strangely endearing. He resisted a shocking urge to catch it in his hand and see if it was as soft as it looked.

She seemed different this morning. Not scatterbrained or desperate to please. She moved about the kitchen with confidence and a simple grace he found appealing. Maybe he had misjudged her. He'd heard only praise about her from his uncle and cousins yesterday at supper.

He needed to get going, but something held him in place. "I wouldn't mind a cup."

She looked surprised but nodded toward the cupboard. "Help yourself while I finish these."

After locating a pair of cups, he poured them both some coffee from the pot on the back of the stove. "Are you making those to take to work?"

"I am." She looked at him, her eyes full of quick concern. "Do you mind?"

"I see no harm in it. If it makes our workers happy, all the better. My uncle says a happy man does the best work."

She smiled. "I think he is right."

He took a seat at the table. It pleased him that he had made her smile. "You know you already have the job. You don't have to impress anyone by supplying us with food."

She drizzled icing over the cooling buns and put one onto a plate. She put it in front of him. "I may not need to impress you, but I do need to apologize for yesterday morning. I'm sure you know my aunt was repeating something she heard from me."

"Do you mean the part when she said I was rude, judgmental and annoying?" He took a bite of the roll.

Helen's cheeks blossomed with bright red spots of color. "*Ja*, that part."

"This is *wunderbarr*," he said with his mouth full. The bread was warm and stuffed with plump, sweet raisins—just the way he liked it.

"*Danki.*" She waited with her hands clasped together. "I hope you can forgive my impertinence. It was mean-spirited of me."

"I might forgive you if you give me a half dozen of these." He took another bite.

Her mouth dropped open. She snapped it shut and huffed, actually huffed, at him. Then a reluctant grim curved her lips. "Rude, judgmental, annoying and greedy. I'll fix you a box to take them home in." She turned away and missed his smile. He liked the way her eyes crinkled at the corners when she was amused.

"*Guder mariye*, Mark Bowman," Charlotte said from the doorway. "What has the two of you grinning like a pair of cats licking the cream?"

The easy comradery Helen was enjoying with Mark vanished under her aunt's questioning gaze.

Charlotte clasped her hands together. "Mark, have you found Juliet?"

He shook his head. "*Nee*, I've not seen her."

"He brought Clyde home again," Helen said. "Did you let him out of your room last night?"

"Did I? I don't think so."

"How could he get out of the house unless you let him out? Perhaps you forgot that you opened the front door for some reason," Mark suggested.

Charlotte pressed her lips together and

shook her head. "I didn't open the front door, and I didn't open the back door. I did open my bedroom window. He must have gone out that way."

Helen looked at Mark. "The window is much too high for him to jump out."

"He got out somehow." Mark took another bite of his delicious roll. They were about the best he'd ever had.

Charlotte smiled at Mark. "I'm mighty glad Clyde fetched you here in time to join us for breakfast. He's a very sociable fellow. When he likes a person, he can't keep it a secret." She moved to the cupboard and took down a cup and plate for herself.

Clyde left his empty bowl and sat beside Mark with his eyes fixed on the remaining half of the cinnamon roll on Mark's plate. He woofed once then planted his front feet on Mark's leg and tried to grab it. Mark yanked the prize away before Clyde's teeth made contact.

"See how much he likes you," Charlotte said in delight.

Mark scowled as the dog sank back to the floor with his eyes still fixed on the plate in Mark's hand. "I see how much he likes my food. He has mighty poor manners."

Clyde seemed to sense he wasn't going to

get anything from Mark. He padded around the table to Charlotte's chair. She bent to take the dog's face between her hands and rub his wrinkled face. "You are a fine *hund*. Even Mark says so."

Helen caught Mark's look of disbelief and shrugged. "Aenti, would you like a cinnamon bun, too?"

Charlotte clapped her hands like a delighted child. "*Danki*, I dreamed about them all night long. It's so kind of you to make them for me. I could bake them myself, but I think food always tastes better when someone else makes it with love. Don't you agree, Mark?"

"If the same recipe and the same ingredients are used, I don't see how the taste could vary." He rose and pushed in his chair. "I have to get to work. Please make sure that Clyde stays at home tonight."

Charlotte glanced at the clock on the wall. "It is getting late. Helen, you must hurry and get ready. You don't want to keep Mark waiting."

"Waiting for what?" he asked, a perplexed look on his face.

"Why, to give Helen a ride to work, of course. That's why you stopped by, isn't it? So very thoughtful of you."

"You don't need to wait for me," Helen said quickly.

Charlotte rose from the table. "Of course he does. How can he take you to work if he doesn't wait? Hurry along, dear. I'll box up your rolls. It was very sweet of you to go out of your way for my niece, Mark. I'll be sure and mention to Isaac and Anna what kindness you've shown her." She opened a cupboard and pulled out some plastic containers.

Mark sighed heavily. "I'm happy to do it. If Helen will hurry up."

She pulled off her apron and dashed toward her room at the back of the house. In record time, she had her hair in a bun that wasn't quite straight but would have to do. Pinning her *kapp* in place, she pulled on a clean white apron and hurried back to the kitchen. Mark wasn't there.

A sharp stab of disappointment surprised her. It couldn't be that she was eager to spend more time with him. That was ridiculous. She didn't even like him.

Okay, she liked him a little. "I guess he got tired of waiting and left without me."

"*Nee*, I had him carry the rolls out. He's waiting for you in the buggy. Have a nice day, dear, and do ask everyone to keep a lookout for Juliet. I can't imagine why she hasn't come home."

Tears shimmered in her aunt's eyes. Helen gave her a hug and kissed her cheek. "We'll find her. Don't give up hope."

"I won't, for I know the Lord cares for all His creatures. Run along. I don't think Mark likes to be kept waiting. If I didn't know better, I'd think he was annoyed with us."

Helen hurried out the door, knowing her aunt was right for a change.

Mark drummed the fingers of his left hand on the armrest of his door. His buggy horse tossed her head, sensing his eagerness to be off, but he held her in check. Finally, Helen climbed in on the passenger's side. He slapped the reins, and the mare lunged ahead. Helen fell against the seat back with a tiny shriek.

"Sorry." He guided his horse down the lane and onto the highway, taking the corner fast enough to send Helen toppling against him.

"Sorry," he said again as she righted herself and scooted away. He urged the horse to a faster pace.

Helen straightened her *kapp*. "You can stop here."

"Why?"

"Because we are out of Aenti Charlotte's sight and I'd like to get to work in one piece."

He scowled at her. "Are you criticizing my driving?"

Helen braced her hands against the dash. "I know you're upset, but please slow down."

"Why would I be upset? Because that ridiculous dog woke me in the middle of the night two nights in a row? Because your *narrish aenti* has decided to play matchmaker between us?"

"Matchmaker? What are you talking about?"

"Anyone with half a brain could see what she was doing. She practically forced me to take you up in my buggy."

"She did not."

"If we are seen riding together there will be talk."

"Now you are being ridiculous."

"Am I? You and the dozen other single women who have descended on Bowmans Crossing this summer are husband hunting and everyone knows it."

"I can't speak for anyone else, but I am not. I repeat, I am *not* looking for a husband." She smacked her fist against her chest. "I intend to earn my own living."

"Ha!"

She crossed her arms and glared at him.

"What's wrong with a woman wanting an independent life?"

"Nothing, if she can't get a man to marry her."

She sucked in an audible breath and turned her face away. He'd hit a nerve. "Oh, I see how it is. You had a beau but he decided he was better off without you. Smart man."

"I don't wish to discuss it."

"I imagine he's celebrating his escape."

"Did it ever occur to you that maybe I called it off?" The catch in her voice stung his conscience. She was on the verge of tears, and he was being a lout.

He slowed his horse and brought the buggy to a stop. She had been crying the first time he saw her, and he didn't believe it was because she had broken it off with some fellow. "I'm sorry, Helen. My words were cruel. I don't know what came over me. I'm not normally like this."

She cleared her throat. "Lack of sleep might be the culprit. That would make me grumpy."

"You are kind to offer me an excuse, but I'm in the wrong, and I beg your forgiveness."

She wiped her cheek with one hand and sniffed. "You are forgiven."

He sat quietly for a long moment, wondering what to say next and how to regain the ease that had existed between them earlier. He glanced at her, seated beside him with her head bowed. "Your aunt is eccentric."

That coaxed a smile from her. "Tell me something I don't know. Now you understand why I must have a job. I want to get a place of my own, and the sooner the better."

"Are you sure she doesn't have matchmaking on her mind?"

"She has informed me that you have a girlfriend back in Pennsylvania, but your brother is free, so I don't think matchmaking between us is her intent. However, I can't be sure of anything where she is concerned except that she loves her silly dog, and she is worried half to death about Juliet."

He didn't have a girl back home anymore. He was tempted to tell Helen about Angela's letter, but he squashed the impulse. "Any thoughts on how to find the raccoon?"

She glanced at him. "I hoped you would have some ideas."

"I think I can come up with a workable plan. First, you should ask the folks at the workshop to keep a lookout for her. All of them live in this area. Then, I will have Jessica make some lost-pet flyers. We can post them around the neighborhood and at other businesses."

"That's a fine notion."

"Where was she last seen?"

"At my aunt's house the evening after the frolic."

"We should concentrate our flyers and searches at the houses closest to yours and then work outward."

"*Danki*. From the bottom of my heart, I mean that."

"For what?"

"For taking Juliet's disappearance seriously."

He clicked his tongue to get the horse moving again. "Don't give me too much credit. I have a selfish motive. If we find Juliet, then maybe Clyde will stay home and let me get a good night's sleep."

"I promise I will do everything in my power to see that he stays home from now on."

"I'm going to hold you to that. Why do you think he keeps coming to my uncle's house?"

"Who knows? Maybe he truly likes you and wants your attention."

"If that's the case, I'll have to prove to him that I'm not a likable fellow."

"How do you intend to do that?"

"I have no idea."

They rounded the curve by the school, and the bridge came into view. He slowed the horse. The ride was almost over, but he wanted to know more about Helen Zook. He'd never met anyone quite like her. "Are you planning on staying in this area?"

"That depends if I can support myself here."

"My uncle pays a fair wage."

"He does. I'm not complaining."

"But you would like to earn more."

"If I continued to live with Charlotte, the pay would be more than adequate, but she doesn't want me there. She says she enjoys living alone."

"So there's a good chance that you'll return home?"

"*Nee*, I will not be going home."

"That sounds final. Were things really that bad?"

She was silent for a long time. He waited, hoping she would confide in him.

She sighed deeply. "I was engaged to be married. A week before the banns were to be announced, my fiancé told my family in front of our bishop that he wanted to marry my sister instead of me. They were married a few days ago. As long as they are there, I won't go home."

It pleased him that she trusted him enough to share her story. Now he understood her tears. "That must have been a difficult time for you."

"You can't imagine how humiliating it was."

"That's the reason you were crying on the bus."

She nodded. "It should have been my wedding day."

"I reckon that was as good a reason as any for tears. Do you still love him?"

"Honestly, I'm not sure how I feel about him except to say I feel betrayed. By both of them."

"Have you forgiven them?"

"I want to say that I have, but I can't. Not yet."

It was a very honest answer, and his respect for her grew. "The time will come when you can say it and mean it."

"I pray that is true."

They came through the bridge and out the other side. He had been wishing the ride could be longer, but perhaps it was best that it wasn't. He was starting to like Helen Zook a little too much.

To his chagrin, Paul was standing beside the front door when they pulled up. His brother's eyebrows rose sharply when Helen stepped out of the buggy.

Helen turned to thank Mark and was taken aback by the deep scowl on his face. He hadn't been angry a few seconds ago. What had changed?

"Good morning, *bruder*. I see you got the dog home safely. Good morning, Helen."

The hint of suppressed laughter in Paul's voice made her realize why Mark was upset. He suspected that Paul would jump to the wrong conclusion because she was riding alone with Mark, and it appeared he was right.

She raised her chin. "Good morning, Paul. You brother was kind enough to give me a ride to work after he returned Clyde this morning. I'm sorry Charlotte's dog is raising havoc. It won't happen again."

"If Mark doesn't mind, I don't." Paul's smile was a bit too flirtatious for Helen's liking.

"I do mind, and I've made that clear, haven't I, Helen?" Mark's stern tone marked an end to the pleasant ride.

"Very clear." She was sorry she had confided in him only a few minutes ago. The sympathetic man who had listened and understood her hurt had vanished. Perhaps he'd only been practicing his listening skill again, and now he was back to his normal self.

"I'll be in as soon as I put the horse and buggy away," Mark said and drove off without a backward glance.

Paul's teasing smile vanished. "I hope my brother wasn't too hard on you."

"Not at all."

"He can be single-minded, and he sometimes forgets other people have feelings, but he has a good heart. I'm happy he didn't scare you away from us. I think you'll enjoy working here."

Would she? With Mark blowing hot and cold, it might not be a comfortable position to be in.

She walked into the office and put her container of rolls on the corner of the small desk that had been moved in since she left last night. It wobbled beneath her hand. The desk had seen better days. It was well-worn with deep scratches in the top surface and scuff marks on the legs. When she tried to open the only drawer, she found it stuck, and she had to use both hands to pull it free.

"A temporary desk for a temporary worker. Message received, Mark Bowman," she muttered drily.

"Are you talking to yourself?"

Her pulse took a jump at the sound of Mark's voice. She spun around to see him in the doorway.

"I was," she admitted.

"You'll have to be careful or some people will think you're as odd as your aunt."

"Some people might be right. I thought you were putting the horse away."

"Rebecca, my cousin Samuel's wife, caught me before I unhitched. She needed to go into town this morning. I see Paul found you a desk." He leaned against it and noticed the wobble. "In a shop that makes furniture, you'd think Paul could find something better than this."

Inordinately pleased that Mark hadn't chosen it for her, she shrugged. "It's fine. I can put a piece of cardboard under the foot to keep it level."

He took a step back. "*Nee*, I'll find you another one."

She picked up her container of cinnamon rolls. "While you are doing that, I'll take these to the break room."

"Wait, I get six of them, remember?" His eyes sparkled with mischief.

She smiled, happy to see the return of the friendly Mark but worried the wrong word from her would have him frowning again. She decided she would treat him as she would anyone else and not worry about his moods. She raised her chin defiantly. "Why should I save six for the greedy man who hasn't said he forgives me?"

He nodded in acknowledgment. "You're forgiven. Hand them over before Paul gets into them."

She opened the plastic container. The aroma of fresh-baked bread filled the small office. "Where shall I put them?"

He reached over and took one. "Put them all in the break room. I was only teasing. Let the men enjoy them. Everyone's been working long hours. They deserve a treat."

Helen smiled as she left the office. He wasn't such a bad fellow after all. The fact that he cared about the men working under him proved that. She put the container on the table in the break room and started the coffee before coming back to the office. Jessica had arrived and was wiping down the counter. Mark was licking his fingers.

Helen chuckled. "Did you even taste it or did you swallow it whole?"

Jessica swept a few crumbs into her palm. "He swallowed it whole and didn't even offer me a bite."

Helen giggled. "I left more in the break room, Jessica."

Mark licked his lips. "I tasted it, and it was *wunderbarr*. Have you considered selling some of you baked goods at the farmers' market in Berlin?"

"This is the first I've heard about a farmers' market." Helen wondered if this was something worth looking into.

Jessica dumped the crumbs in the waste basket. "They hold it every Friday afternoon from three o'clock until seven during the spring, summer and fall. In the winter, they hold it every third Friday of the month. There's also a weekly market at Apple Creek although it's smaller. It's held on Tuesday afternoons from three until eight."

Helen turned the idea over in her mind. If she could supplement her income with her baking, that would be wonderful. "The Berlin market, is it big? Is it well attended?"

Mark shrugged. "It's not as large as some of the ones I've attended in Pennsylvania, but it draws a fair-sized crowd. A lot of *Englisch* come each week."

Helen walked to the calendar hanging on the wall. If she started cooking as soon as she got home tonight, she could have plenty of goods to sell. "Every Friday afternoon. Would I be able to get off work to go?"

"If we aren't busy," Mark said. "You could make up your hours by coming in early a couple of days a week or by staying late, if you didn't want to lose pay."

"Count me as a customer," Jessica said with a broad smile. "I always swing by there on my way home and stock up on fresh produce and baked goods for the weekend."

Paul came in and leaned on the counter. "What are we talking about?"

"The farmers' market." Helen turned to Mark. "May I have tomorrow afternoon off?"

He cupped his hand over his chin and tapped his index finger against his lips. "This Friday? Maybe. I'll have to check our freight schedule."

"Okay. Well, I should get to work. I'm only here on probation for a month."

Jessica laughed. "If Mark fires you, come back in two months' time. He'll be long gone to Pennsylvania, and I'll make sure Isaac hires you again."

"You're leaving?" Helen stared at Mark, unable to keep her surprise hidden.

Chapter Eight

So Mark was leaving Bowmans Crossing. Helen wasn't sure how she felt about that. On the one hand, it would be nice to work without him frowning at her every move. On the other hand...

She gave herself a mental shake. There was no other hand. She liked him a little, although she didn't know why. He was gruff and rude, and he had a girl back home. That put him off-limits as surely as if he were married. She would never do to another woman what her sister had done to her. She wasn't interested in a new romantic relationship anyway, not after the way Joseph had treated her. She wasn't sure she could trust her heart to another man after that.

Paul moved to stand beside her, his flirty smile once again in place. "My brother may be leaving, but I intend to settle down here and make my home in Bowmans Crossing."

"Then I may have to move," she replied with marked indifference and hoped he got the message that she wasn't interested. She caught Mark's eye as he smothered a grin.

He sobered quickly. "That put you in your place, little brother."

Jessica giggled. "You are wasting your time, Paul. She is too smart to fall for the likes of you."

Paul clasped his hands over his heart. "You wound me, Jessica. If you were Amish, you'd be the only one for me."

"I've seen you go out with non-Amish girls. I'm too smart to fall for the likes of you, too."

Someone cleared his throat, and the group turned to see Isaac standing in the doorway. "If I'm not mistaken, there is work waiting to be done."

Jessica sat down at her computer and turned it on. Paul squeezed past his uncle and went out the door. Helen glanced at Mark and saw his face was beet red. "Forgive my slacking. It was my intent to have the men start on the Fielding projects, but I was…"

"Sidetracked. I can see that," Isaac said, with a pointed look at Helen. "Why don't you help with the Fielding project, Mark, and I'll shadow Helen today."

"I'll do that." He nodded to his uncle and went out.

"I didn't mean to keep the men from their work. It won't happen again," Helen said earnestly.

Isaac chuckled. "It will happen again. Jessica loves to chat."

"True, very true," she said from her desk.

Isaac's smiled fondly at her and shook his head. "Paul finds any excuse to delay getting started in the workshop. He's a slow mover except when he's working as an auctioneer. Then, he's amazingly quick. I fear furniture making isn't his calling. I admit I was surprised to see Mark visiting in here instead of working."

Helen didn't know how to respond. She hadn't meant to distract anyone. "I am going to put these cinnamon rolls in the break room, and then I will be ready to get started. Mark was going to show me how to inventory the different types of wood used here."

Isaac held up a hand to stop her. "Before you go, I'll take one."

"Of course." She opened the plastic container and held it out to him. He took his time selecting which one he wanted.

"I'm not a great fan of raisins."

"The next time I make them, I'll remember that and bring some plain ones."

"You don't have to feed us," he said.

Helen shrugged. "Mark said the same thing. I like to bake, and it's nice to bake for people who appreciate what I make."

"Then far be it for me to discourage you." He stepped aside, and Helen went down the hall to leave her rolls in the break room. Mark was coming out of the supply room with a new circular saw blade in his hand. He passed her without speaking.

"Mark, I'm sorry," she said to his back. She had apologized more to this man than anyone in her life. Was God still trying to teach her a lesson in humility?

Mark stopped. "It wasn't your fault."

"He's not angry with you."

"I disappointed him. It won't happen again." He walked away without looking at her.

Later in the morning, Helen was making notes as Isaac went over the different types of plywood they kept on hand and their uses. After counting the stacks of three-ply, five-ply and cabinet-grade plywood, she finally had to say something.

"If you feel that Mark is distracted because of me, I can look for employment elsewhere."

Isaac scratched his beard. "Are you distracting Mark?"

"Not on purpose, but we have had some unusual encounters."

"Such as?"

Helen was sorry she had broached the subject. Should she mention they had met on the bus? Had Mark told anyone about her? "My aunt's dog has been annoying Mark in the middle of the night. Twice he has had to bring the dog home."

"Charlotte's dog has been annoying the entire household."

"I know, and I'm sorry. Mark feels he disappointed you this morning, and I wanted you to know the reason why Mark brought me to work with him today."

He tipped his head to the side. "I wasn't aware that Mark brought you to work."

"My aunt forced him to bring me. It's a long story. Perhaps I should stop talking now and go back to counting types of plywood."

"Your desire to defend Mark is admirable. I certainly am not disappointed in Mark. I was pleasantly surprised to see him socializing. He is normally something of a loner."

"He values your opinion. If you are not upset with him, I wish you would let him know that."

"I will, and thank you for the reminder. I seldom praise the men here for a job well-done, and I should do so more often. It's almost lunchtime. We can resume this count after we eat. My wife has asked that you join us for lunch."

"I would be delighted."

"Then I will see you up at the house, but first I must speak with Mark."

As they went back through the workshop, Helen saw all the men, save Mark, had turned off their machines and were heading outside to enjoy the lunches their wives or mothers had packed for them. One man rode off on his bicycle. Helen assumed he lived close enough to go home for lunch.

Isaac crossed the room to speak with Mark. Helen went into the office and found Jessica texting on her cell phone. She grinned at Helen and held the device in the air. "This is the number one reason I could never be Amish. I don't know how you do without one."

"I can't miss what I have never had."

"I guess that's true. Are you eating here, or are you going to go home?"

"I've been invited up to the house."

"Have you met Anna?"

"Briefly, at the frolic." Helen would rather

forget about that day. She was glad Jessica hadn't been in attendance.

"You will like her. She's a hoot."

"I wanted you to know that I was leaving." Helen waved goodbye and stepped out into the workroom. Isaac was already gone. Mark was shutting down his machine. She started to leave, but he called her name.

She waited for him to catch up as a flock of butterflies took flight in her stomach.

Mark reached Helen's side and held open the door for her to go out ahead of him. He wanted to thank her, but he wasn't sure how to put into words what he was feeling. They walked toward the house in silence until they reach the front door. He caught her arm before she went in. "Why did you tell my uncle I felt that I'd let him down?"

"I knew you were upset, and I wanted to make it right since it was partly my fault. Your uncle told you he wasn't disappointed, didn't he?"

"He's not a man who gives compliments freely, so when he tells you that you have done a *goot* job he means it." For Mark, the warm glow of his uncle's praise was still centered in his chest. He knew he had been working hard, but to hear his uncle express his admiration was akin to winning a hard-fought race.

"I'm glad." She gave him a shy smile that made his pulse jump a notch higher. Why did she have this effect on him? He scowled as he tried to understand what it was that she was doing. Her smiled faded, and she rushed through the door.

During the meal, he found it hard to keep his eyes off Helen. She conversed easily with Anna and Rebecca. The tale of Juliet's disappearance had everyone speculating about what could have happened to the raccoon. The consensus among the men was that she had returned to the wild, but most of the women disagreed. Twelve-year-old Hannah and her mother, Mary, promised to keep an eye out for Juliet when they were out in the rowboat fishing on the river, an activity they both enjoyed. The story of Charlotte accusing the bishop's wife and then Mark of dognapping had everyone chuckling.

Occasionally, Helen glanced his way, and he noticed a slight rise in the color of her cheeks each time she met his gaze. He had never been interested in a woman enough to want to find out more about her until now. There were many things he wanted to learn about Helen. Did she have a big family? What kind of books did she enjoy? What kind of man had been engaged to her and chose another woman instead?

She smiled at something Samuel said, and Mark noticed the color and shape of her lips for the first time. Try as he might, he couldn't recall Angela's lips. Were they narrow or full like Helen's? Were they the color of pink rosebuds, or were they pale?

Paul kicked the side of Mark's foot. He glared at his brother. "What?"

"You're staring," Paul whispered.

"I was not." Mark looked down at his plate. "Did she notice?"

"I don't think so."

He glanced at Helen once more. She was talking to his cousin Timothy's wife, Lillian. Helen happened to glance his way, but he quickly looked down. He folded his napkin and rose to his feet. "I forgot something in the shop."

"Don't you want some gooseberry pie for dessert?" Anna asked. "It's your favorite."

"Save some for me. I'll have it later." He walked away without looking at Helen, until he reached the front door. When he glanced back, she was watching him. He ducked his head and left the house.

Ten minutes later, Paul stopped beside him

in the workroom. "Is there something you want to tell me?"

"I need another sheet of three ply," he said without looking up from the dresser he was building.

"If I didn't know better, I'd say you are smitten with Helen."

"Have you seen the hand sander?"

"Samuel is using it, and you are trying to change the subject."

Mark sighed loudly and looked at Paul. "What subject would that be?"

"Whether or not you are smitten with the very attractive Helen Zook."

"I'm not. Do you think she's pretty?"

"Very. Don't you?"

"I hadn't noticed. Are you gonna get me that three ply, or do I have to get it myself?"

"I'll get it. Just be careful, that's all I'm saying."

"I'm always careful around power tools."

Paul leaned in to look Mark in the eyes. "I wasn't referring to power tools. A broken heart can't be fixed with nails and glue."

"You're being ridiculous. I've only just met her. No one's heart is in jeopardy. Least of all mine."

"For your sake I hope that's true." Paul walked away.

Mark laid down his hammer. Paul had it all wrong. Even if he was attracted to Helen, which he wasn't, he told himself sternly, she was not the kind of woman he needed. She made him feel as if his skin was too tight. How could a man be comfortable with a woman like that?

For the first time since receiving Angela's letter, Mark considered trying to win her back. It would solve so many problems. Her father would sell him the land he wanted. He wouldn't have to start over and find a new place to build his business. He wouldn't have to deal with dating women to find one who would suit his needs.

He would write Angela's father and ask if he knew why she had changed her mind. He would get his plan back on track, and then he would forget about Helen Zook.

The moment she got home from work, Helen pushed all thoughts of Mark out of her mind as she threw her heart and soul into baking. Charlotte, although disappointed that there wasn't any sign of Juliet, joined Helen in the kitchen, and the two of them were soon elbow deep in dough. By midnight, they had eight loaves of bread, three decorated cakes, two dozen assorted crescent rolls, three dozen frosted cupcakes, six dozen cookies and four pies. Two peach and two gooseberry, because Anna had said it was Mark's favorite.

Happily, Clyde stayed at home that night, so there was no early-morning visit from Mark. Helen slept later than she intended and had to rush to get to work on time. Charlotte promised to pack up the food and a table to display it on and pick Helen up at one o'clock. That would give them enough time to get to Berlin, pay the booth-rental fee and get set up before the market opened at three.

At work, Helen was eager to share her idea with Mark, but every time she approached him he took off in another direction. He seemed so busy she started to wonder if he was avoiding her. She settled for discussing her plans with Jessica, who was wonderfully supportive.

Keeping busy until it was time to leave wasn't a problem. A shipment of hardware came in at ten o'clock and it took her the rest of the morning to put it away in the assigned drawers. Twice, Mark came in to get something but didn't speak to her.

To her utter relief, Charlotte showed up as promised and without Clyde. Helen had persuaded her that it would be hard to keep the dog safe with so much traffic in town. Rather than risk losing another pet, Charlotte had shut Clyde in her bedroom.

They found where the market was to be held and located the man taking booth fees. Because she was the last person to pay for a spot, Helen was given a booth at the far end of the grassy lot. After rushing to get set up and get her wares on the table, Helen was finally able to take a deep breath and relax for a few minutes after three. The tree-lined green space at the park was lined on both sides with tents and colorful awnings. Fresh fruit and vegetables were displayed in wooden cases stacked on bales of straw or on tables. People strolled down the avenue with bags for carrying their purchases or even small wheeled carts.

As she scanned the approaching shoppers, she noticed Mark sitting beneath the shade of an oak tree across the way. He rose and strolled over to her table.

She smiled brightly. "Good afternoon. Can I interest you in some baked goods, sir? All fresh from the oven."

"So, what is your plan? What business model are you working from?"

Her smile slipped a little. "My plan is to sell all my baked goods and go home with extra money in my pocket. I don't know what a business model is, and I don't want to know. Would you care to buy a pie? I have gooseberry."

"Maybe later. I'm going to look around first, and I don't have a place to leave a pie. Are you giving away free samples?"

"*Nee*, if you want to see what it tastes like, you'll have to buy it."

"That might be a mistake."

Her patience vanished. "If you aren't going to buy anything, please move along so others can see what we have."

He tipped his hat and walked away. She turned to Charlotte, who was sitting on a folding chair behind the table munching on a cookie. "Aenti, those are for sale, not for snacking."

"I forgot." Charlotte slipped the half-eaten cookie back underneath the plastic wrap and returned the package to the table.

When Helen was sure Mark was out of earshot, she spoke to her aunt. "Do you know what a business model is?"

"I believe those are the women who wear tiny swimsuits and have their pictures in a magazine. Shameful, if you ask me. You don't want to be one of those. The bishop would forbid it."

Helen was sure that Mark hadn't been referring to women in swimsuits. "Why don't you finish your cookie?"

"Oh, may I? *Danki*, my dear." She snatched up the package and unwrapped it.

Helen fixed a smile on her face and waited for the patrons to make their way to her end of the market. She had made one sale, a dozen chocolate chip cookies, by the time Mark returned an hour later. It wasn't enough to cover her booth rental.

"How are you doing?" he asked.

"If things don't pick up, I will lose money instead of making it. Good food should sell itself."

"Does anyone here know you're a good baker?"

"I do," Charlotte said, waving her hand in the air.

"Besides your *aenti*?" He covered his mouth with his hand.

Helen's patience was wearing thin. "What are you doing here?"

"Moral support. I suggested this, and I wanted to see how it worked out for you. I was afraid you hadn't had enough time to adequately prepare."

"It's working out just fine. You may go home now."

He pointed toward the far end of the market.

"There is a bakery booth down there that's doing a brisk business."

She let out a huff of disgust. "Pour salt in my wound why don't you."

"I'm telling you this so you can see your mistakes and correct them. If you had done a little research—"

"Go away."

He shook a finger at her. "That was rude. I'm trying to help."

"Please go away."

"All right. I'll be over there if you need me." He turned and walked off. Helen was tempted to throw a gooseberry pie at him but thought better of it. Such a display of temper was sure to turn potential customers away.

Three hours later, Helen stared at everything she had to pack in the buggy again. Besides the cookies, she had sold one loaf of bread and one pie to Jessica. No one had purchased her beautifully decorated cakes and she'd sold only one dozen cupcakes. Discouraged didn't begin to describe how she felt.

And to have Mark witness her failure made it even worse. He left his shade tree and came over. "Can I help you pack up?"

"If you must."

Charlotte carried a box with a cake in it to the buggy. "Look at it this way, dear. We won't have to bake anything to take to the church service on Sunday. We can spend the entire day tomorrow looking for Juliet."

"Let's hope we have more success at that than I had today."

"Your cookies were delicious." Charlotte had consumed a half dozen.

Mark folded the table and slid it in the back seat of Helen's buggy. "What did you learn about selling at a local market today?"

"That it was a waste of time and money. I wish you'd never said anything about it." Helen climbed in the buggy and jiggled the reins to get the horse moving. She couldn't wait to put this unsuccessful experience behind her.

Anna Bowman was working in the kitchen when Mark came in the house after returning from Berlin. He set two jars of jam that he had purchased at the market on the counter. "I thought you might like these. The little jar is lavender jam, and the tall pink one is rose-petal jam."

"How interesting. Would you like to try some now?"

"I'd rather not be the guinea pig. Ask Noah. He'll eat anything."

Anna laughed softly. "I like this change in you, Mark."

He leaned against the counter beside her. "What change?"

"You never used to joke around. You were always so serious, even as a little boy when you stayed with us that year."

It had been the summer after his mother died. Mark's dad hadn't been able to care for him and had sent a sad, lonely little boy to live with Anna and Isaac, the aunt and uncle he'd never met. Fortunately, he soon fell in love with the entire family. They were everything his family wasn't. "Maybe Paul's antics are beginning to rub off on me."

"How did Helen fare at the market?"

"Not well, and I feel responsible. It was my suggestion, but she took the idea and ran with it without any kind of plan or forethought. She wasted her time and money. She wants to get a place of her own, but it won't happen if she keeps on the same path. She's so impulsive. I don't know what to do with her."

"That's too bad."

"What do you think about Helen selling some of her goods in your gift shop?"

"I don't see why not. We already sell jams and candy and other food stuffs. Some home-made Amish bread might sell well if we pair it with a discounted jar of jam. It's nice of you to try and help Helen."

He shifted from one foot to the other. "I'm not sure she thinks so."

"Perhaps her pride is getting in the way."

"She thinks she has to succeed on her own."

"No one succeeds without help along the way, both from Heaven and from our friends and family on earth. You like her, don't you, Mark?"

"Maybe. She leaves me feeling all tied up inside."

"And Angela?"

"Angela doesn't make me feel like a fool or a brute or both at the same time."

Anna cupped his face between her hands. "You are neither a brute nor a fool. I'm going to miss you when you go back to Pennsylvania."

"I'll write and come visit often."

"*Goot.* I look forward to meeting your Angela."

If there was anyone he could confide in, it was Anna. "She may not be my Angela anymore."

"What? Why is that?"

"Her last letter said she has decided she doesn't wish to marry me."

"Mark, I'm so sorry. Did she say why?"

"*Nee.*"

"What are you going to do? You must go home at once and find out what is wrong. The two of you have been corresponding for ages. I thought the matter had been decided between the two of you."

"I wrote to her father."

"That's not the same as talking to her face-to-face. She has faithfully written to you every week as you have written to her. You should go see her."

"My apprenticeship with Isaac is almost finished. I will stick to my plan and speak to Angela when I go home."

"I pray you know what you are doing."

"I have thought it out, and I believe that's the best course for me."

"Matters of the heart seldom follow the plans *we* make, for it is *Gott's* plan that leads us to our soul mate. Do you pray for His guidance?"

"I do," he answered, but he wondered if he spoke the truth. God hadn't been at the forefront of Mark's life for a long time. His focus was on what he wanted and how he could achieve that.

His aunt's words stayed with him all evening and even after he said his prayers and climbed into bed. In his determination to fashion the life he had dreamed of as a child, he'd lost sight of the importance of prayer. What if God had a different plan for his life? How would he face that? Could he accept it? How did he know what God wanted him to do?

After a fitful first half of the night, Mark had finally drifted off to sleep when a mournful howl brought him wide awake. Fuming, Mark sat up and looked at his clock. It was three thirty. "That miserable dog! I'm not hauling him home again!"

He flopped back and covered his head with his pillow, but it didn't help. The deep baying penetrated even that barrier.

Mark threw back the covers and noticed his slippers at the side of the bed when he sat up. He snatched one and crossed to the window. He spied movement in the darkness below.

"Go home!" he shouted and threw the shoe. "Ow!"

Startled to hear a woman's voice, he leaned farther out the window. "Helen?"

Chapter Nine

Sitting on the ground beside Clyde's tree, Helen held both hands over her stinging left eye, trying not to cry.

"Helen, are you okay?" She heard Mark's voice above her.

The pain was so intense she couldn't open her eyes. "*Nee*, I can't see."

"Stay still. I'll be right down."

"Oh, great," she muttered. This was exactly what she had hoped to avoid. Clyde proceeded to lick her ear and bark eagerly. She pushed him away. "Stop. This is all your fault."

By the time Mark reached her side the pain had eased some, but she still couldn't open her eyes without the discomfort returning, so she kept them tightly closed. He grasped her by the shoulders. "What's wrong, Helen?"

"Something hit me in the eye."

"I'm afraid it was my slipper. What are you doing here?"

His slipper? "Why did you throw your slipper out the window?"

"I was aiming at the dog. Not aiming exactly, but I was trying to scare him into going home."

She peeked with her good eye. Clyde was dancing around them, happily wagging his tail and darting in to lick her ear then trying to lick Mark, who pushed him away. "He doesn't look scared to me," she said drily.

"Helen," Mark said slowly. "What are you doing here in the middle of the night?"

"I was trying to stop Clyde from waking you, but I got here too late."

"Why don't you start at the beginning."

"I heard a commotion outside my aunt's home. When I looked out my window, I saw Clyde disappearing into the woods in this direction. I got dressed, grabbed his leash and got on my bicycle to try and get here before him. I didn't know he could run so fast. I mean, look at him! He's all flab, and he has little stubby legs, but he got here first and started howling before I could grab his collar. I heard you yell, and I looked up. The next thing I know something hit me in the eye."

"I'm so sorry."

Helen struggled to her feet. "I know it was an accident. We seem to have a lot of them, you and me."

"That is an understatement. I'll get the buggy and take you home."

She managed to keep her eye open for a few seconds before she had to squint again. "I don't need a ride. My bicycle is up on the road. Would you snap the leash on Clyde, please?"

"You can't ride a bike and manage Clyde, too." He fastened the lead and handed it to her.

"I'll walk him home. The sound of a horse and buggy driving up to the house might wake Charlotte. I'd rather avoid that." Helen climbed up the slope leading to the road with one eye open. She looped Clyde's leash around the handlebars and started for the bridge. He wasn't in the mood to go and nearly jerked the bike out of her hands as he tried to dart back to his tree. "Clyde, please, I just want to go home."

"Let me have him." Mark had followed her and stood with his hand out.

She sighed and untied the dog. "Okay."

Mark took it, and Clyde immediately sat beside him looking up with what she could only describe as an expression of doggy admiration. She cupped her hand over her stinging eye again. "I think Charlotte is right. He likes you."

"I'm so honored."

Helen had to chuckle at his sarcasm. "Imagine how boring this week would have been without Clyde. I wouldn't have almost run you over with a buggy."

"I wouldn't have taken a dive into a mud puddle."

"And you wouldn't have been wearing my delicious cream horns on your shirt front."

"You wouldn't have tried to burn your aunt's house down. Did you locate the fire extinguisher?"

"I did. Without Clyde, I wouldn't have a shoe print on my face." The pain was almost gone. She could keep both eyes open if she squinted.

"Let me see." He leaned forward to see her face by the light of the moon. "Your eye may be red for a while, but I don't think it will leave a mark."

"If it does, I'm telling everyone at church on Sunday that you stepped on my face."

"You wish to get me shunned?" he asked in outrage.

"*Nee*, I wouldn't. I'm only teasing."

"I know, so am I," he said with a grin. She smiled softly in return and started walking again.

He stared after her. He'd never teased or been teased by a woman before. He'd certainly never spent a moonlit night walking a girl home. Helen's presence had become comfortable in a way he hadn't thought possible. Maybe it was because she wasn't looking for husband. He didn't have to worry that his attention would be mistaken. He liked the idea of having her as a friend.

Clyde jerked on the lead, forcing Mark to stumble forward. As soon as he caught up with Helen, Clyde stopped pulling and walked quietly beside him.

Mark stared at the dog and stood still again. Once Helen was a few steps ahead, Clyde started pulling on his lead. When Mark caught up with her, Clyde ambled quietly beside Mark, occasionally bumping against his leg, forcing him to move closer to Helen. "This is a strange dog."

"He gets it from Charlotte. She talks to him like he understands what she is saying."

"Do you think he does?"

She shot him a look of disbelief. "He's a dog, Mark."

"Yeah, you're right. He's just a dog." Wasn't he?

Clyde wagged his tail and woofed once.

"What are you going to do with your left-over baked goods?" he asked to change the subject.

"I will take some to church on Sunday and freeze some. I'll take the rest to the shop on Monday. Charlotte and I can't eat them all."

"Aenti Anna said you are welcome to sell some baked goods at her gift shop."

"I'll think about it."

"You are giving up too easily."

"I'm not giving up," she insisted. "I know I can turn a profit if others can. I need to start small and work my way up."

"You failed to make a profit on your first attempt, but that isn't unusual for a new business venture. You made some beginner mistakes." Mark found himself on familiar ground. He knew the ins and outs of business, and he didn't mind sharing that knowledge.

"And now you're going to tell me what they were?" Helen asked. "It might have been helpful if you had told me beforehand."

"I didn't tell you because you didn't ask. You have enthusiasm, but your approach lacks common sense. You overestimated the amount you could reasonably sell because you didn't do your research. You failed to identify who your customers are, and you failed to study your competition. A well-thought-out business plan is important before you take the first step of investing time and energy. That's why you didn't do well."

She started walking faster. "I can't thank you enough for pointing out my shortcomings."

"You're quite welcome. We can all learn from our mistakes."

"My mistake was letting you walk me home." She sounded angry, and he didn't know why.

"I don't understand."

Helen stopped in her tracks. "I don't need a lecture from you."

"I thought you wanted my advice."

She fisted her hands on her hips. "You thought wrong. Since you seem to know so much about business, why don't you come up with a plan that will work?"

"For you?"

"*Ja*, for me. I'd like to see you figure out everything I need to do to turn a profit. Since you are a furniture maker and not a baker, I don't believe you can do any better than I did."

"It would be difficult to do worse."

She made that huffing sound that told him

he should've stopped talking a while back. She got on her bike and began to pedal away from him. He had to jog to catch up. She pedaled faster.

He was winded by the time they reached her aunt's house. He bent over with his hands braced on his knees to catch his breath. Clyde flopped to the ground, panting heavily.

Helen took the dog's lead from Mark's hand. "Thank you for escorting me home. Good night."

"I'll do it," he wheezed.

"What?"

"I'll come up with a business plan for you," he said between deep breaths, wondering why he felt compelled to help someone who clearly didn't want it.

"Don't bother." She tugged Clyde up the porch steps.

Mark straightened, ignoring the stitch in his side. "It's no bother."

She entered the house and shut the door without answering.

Sunday, after the three-hour church service and a midday meal, Helen sat beside Fannie and Rebecca Bowman, watching the young people enjoying a game of volleyball. Helen had given up playing after her baptism. She missed the friendly competitions, but she was happy in the company of her new friends. It was nice to relax and have a conversation with young women near her own age.

Fannie nibbled on one of Helen's cream cheese–stuffed crescent rolls. "How is your job going? Do you like it?"

Helen shrugged. "It's okay. I'm learning a lot about wood and tools."

Rebecca held the hand of her toddler as the boy walked with shaky steps to Fannie. "Samuel tells me you're catching on quickly."

"I'm happy someone thinks so. I'm afraid Mark isn't of the same opinion. He's the most arrogant man I have ever met!" Helen rubbed her left eye. It was better, but Mark's comments about her shortcomings still rankled.

"Don't take Mark's cool attitude personally," Rebecca said. "Samuel said he's been like that all his life. He thinks it's because Mark's mother died when he was so young, and his father had trouble taking care of him. Mark ended up being shuffled from one family to the next while his father searched for work. The poor child never stayed anywhere more than a few months until he came to live with Isaac and Anna. They refused to send Mark back to his father until he had a steady job. Mark lived here for two years. His father eventually remarried and settled down, but by then Mark didn't want to go back."

"Did he stay here?" Helen asked, more interested than she cared to admit.

"His father insisted he come home. Isaac and Anna gave in but not before a lot of tears were shed."

"What about Paul?" Fannie asked.

Rebecca held out her hands to her son. He grinned and bounced on Fannie's lap. "Paul and Mark aren't related by blood. Paul's mother was a widow with a young son when she married Mark's father. They had five children together, so Mark and Paul each have five younger half siblings."

Fannie held the baby's fingers while he took steps back to Rebecca. "Paul and Mark act like brothers."

"They do," Helen agreed. She looked across the lawn to where Mark stood in conversation with Bishop Beachy, Samuel and Isaac. Mark's story gave her a little more insight into his personality. Had a childhood of insecurity produced a man who craved order? It made sense. Maybe she needed to be more tolerant of his quirks instead of taking offense.

On Monday, Helen resolved to be pleasant to him, but she had little opportunity to put her resolution into effect, for he worked on carving a new mantelpiece the entire day and left her to manage the supply room alone.

She walked out of the shop a little after four o'clock in the afternoon. Isaac had closed early because many of the men were traveling to a wedding the next day. Mark was sitting in an open-topped buggy outside the front door. He nodded toward the passenger side. "Get in."

She arched one eyebrow. "You forgot to say please."

He closed his eyes and took a deep breath. "Please get in."

She smiled. "See how much more pleasant you sound when you use that one small word?"

"Are you going to get in or not?"

"There's no need for you to take me home. I rode my bike to work."

"I'm not taking you home. I'm taking you to the farmers' market in Apple Creek to see what you did wrong."

His pointed reminder of her failure at the last market crumpled her new resolve. "I didn't bake anything, so I have nothing to sell." She walked past him to where her bicycle was parked.

Mark clicked his tongue to make his mare move up beside her. "You challenged me to come up with a business plan for you."

"And you haven't said a word about it. You barely spoke to me today."

"I was busy. I'm willing to talk about it now. The first rule of business is to know your customer. The second is to know your competition. You have a good product, but you don't know what the demand for it is. You don't know the price point you should set, and you don't know what sells best at a farmers' market."

She folded her arms across her chest. "It was glaringly apparent that I did not know these things. I thought good food would sell itself."

"One way to learn the business without so much painful trial and error is to observe your competition in action. Come on. I can develop a plan for you, but I can't implement it for you."

"Did anyone ever tell you that you don't talk like an Amish person?"

He tipped his head to the side. "What does that mean?"

"You use big, hard-to-understand words."

"I have furthered my education. I'm sorry you don't like the tone of my speech. What words didn't you understand?"

"Implement."

"It means I can't start the plan for you."

"Why don't you say that?"

"Come along with me. Don't you want to see what you did wrong?"

"Maybe."

"I think I know you better than that. I think underneath that I-don't-care exterior, you're dying to give it another go."

How did he know she was itching to try once more? Maybe she wasn't as good at pretending indifference as she thought she was. "You're right. I am."

She rushed around the back of the buggy and climbed into the passenger seat, ignoring the self-satisfied grin on his face.

"That's the spirit." He slapped the reins against the horse's rump and guided her out onto the road. She trotted along at a brisk clip.

Helen gradually relaxed and began to enjoy the ride. It was a lovely spring afternoon. The sun was shining, but a north breeze kept it from becoming too hot. She stole a glance at Mark. "I have to ask. What prompted you to offer me this help?"

He met her gaze. "Your determination. Anyone else would have given up trying to get a job with me after the abject failures you had. It was dogged determination on your part, and I admire that."

"Desperation not determination."

"I don't agree. You encounter a dilemma, and you attack it. Your sister steals your fiancé. You don't hide at home, you set out to make a new life for yourself in another state. You don't want to continue living with your odd aunt. You decided you needed a job, and you kept at it until you were hired."

"Aenti Charlotte was responsible for that."

"Perhaps, but few people would have come to face me after the humiliation you suffered. You wanted to earn extra money, so you decided on a course of action based on sound principles. You enjoy baking, and you're very good at it. Then you put your idea in motion. Your vision suffered a setback, but I don't believe you'll let that stop you. You will try again, and ultimately I think you will succeed."

"You do? You think I will succeed at my own business?"

"We all have a different idea of what success is, but I think you will reach your goal of being able to move out of your aunt's home."

Helen folded her hands together and raised her eyes to heaven. "Please let that be what happens. I love Charlotte, but she and Clyde are a trial to live with."

"Has she always been strange, or is she getting worse because she is getting older?"

"She's always been different, but her obsession with her pets is getting worse. I think she is lonely, but she claims she enjoys living alone."

"Sometimes people say one thing and mean another."

Was he talking about himself or her aunt? She wondered if he was as indifferent to her as he tried to make out. "I have been guilty of that in the past."

"I take it the flyers have not been successful in locating Juliet?"

"One *Englisch* man stopped by to say that he had seen her by the side of the road on the way into town, but he couldn't say for sure that it was Juliet. He wanted to know if there was a reward. I'm not sure he saw anything, but it could've been another raccoon."

"Surely by now your aunt is ready to accept that Juliet might not return."

"*Nee*, she isn't ready to give up. She says she has a hunch that Juliet will turn up."

"A hunch is just a guess," he said softly.

"Or a wish."

Helen had a hunch that Mark was interested in her. Was it a guess or a wish? The last thing she wanted to do was to steal another woman's fiancé. No matter how much she might like Mark, she could never act on those feelings. He wasn't free. She had to keep a lid on her emotions until he left in a few weeks. If she could. He was much too good at reading her feelings.

The ride in the countryside was beautiful. Farmhouses along the way had flowers blooming in abundance in the yards, including colorful tulips and daffodils. The fruit trees were in bloom, and the cattle stood knee-deep in bright green grass.

It wasn't long before the outskirts of the town came into view. Small houses with small lawns gave way to businesses that lined both sides of the streets. He slowed the mare and stopped at a red light. Helen looked around in amazement. "The traffic is much heavier today."

"It will stay this way most of the summer and into the fall. This community is a tourist destination. Bowmans Crossing is still far enough off the beaten path to avoid much of this, but I don't think it will stay that way for long."

He found a place to park and, after leaving his horse with feed and water, he reached up to help Helen get down. The touch of his hand on her arm sent a thrill spiraling through her midsection. He quickly pulled his hand away as if he felt the sensation, too. She pretended to admire the array of tents and canopies that had been set up.

"If I do continue, I will need a canopy."

"Why not a tent?"

"Because I want my food to be on display. I don't want people to walk by because they don't know what's inside."

"*Goot.* Now you are thinking like a businesswoman. Write it down in your notebook."

"How did you know I brought a notebook?" she asked as she extracted it from her bag.

"During your orientation at work, you kept writing in one. I assumed you would want to take notes today."

"I'm not sure I like the way you seem to know what I'm thinking."

"I observe people, and I learn things about them. It's no secret."

"Maybe not, but it's a little creepy."

They walked together down the grassy aisle between the booths. Everything from woven baskets to carved wooden toys and fresh honey was for sale. The booth that was selling baked goods was doing a brisk business.

"What do you see that you like about their setup?" Mark asked.

"The displays are beautiful, and they are tipped at an angle so people can see them better. I had my things arranged flat on the table.

I see they are giving out samples, too. I didn't want to give away my product, but I see now that if people like what they taste, they will purchase more. I also see that my prices were high."

"Folks come to a farmers' market for bargains. Notice what people are buying and what they are eating." Mark tipped his head toward an *Englisch* mother with two small children. The children each had a cookie in their hands.

"Things they can carry and eat as they shop." She noticed cookies and muffins in the hands of several other patrons. No one was carrying two-layer cakes.

"Shall we see what the other food vendors are doing?"

"*Ja*, I'd like to do that. Did you know all these things before you suggested I try selling my goods at a farmers' market?"

"I noticed them while I was watching you last Friday. You weren't selling much. I know your product is good, so there had to be a reason people weren't buying."

"I should have done that instead of being hurt and humiliated that no one wanted my cooking."

"You're doing it now."

"I reckon you can teach this old dog new tricks," she said with a chuckle, and he grinned.

She had made him smile. The satisfaction she felt was far out of proportion to her accomplishment. Movement across the way caught her eye.

"Mark, look, there is another basset hound. Isn't she cute?" Helen walked toward the *Englisch* couple holding the dog's leash. The dog was following her mistress's commands and showing off some tricks, earning treats from a plastic bag.

"I'm not sure I would use the word *cute*," Mark said drily.

"I think she is. I'm going to talk to them."

"Of course you are." Mark tagged along behind her.

She stopped in front of a couple. "Hello. I just had to say what a pretty basset hound you have. What is her name?"

The woman smiled. "She has an AKC-registered name, but we call her Bonnie."

Helen laughed. "My aunt's dog is Clyde."

The woman chuckled. "That is too funny. Bonnie and Clyde. We absolutely must get them together someday for a playdate. Does your aunt live nearby?"

"She lives just past Bowmans Crossing. What is a playdate?"

"It means getting together to let the dogs have some fun. We make a date to let the dogs play together. A playdate."

"Now I've heard of everything," Mark muttered. "Making a date for your dog."

"I think it's a great idea." Helen squatted on her heels to pet Bonnie. "She's so well trained. My aunt's dog is...not so well trained."

Mark pushed the brim of his hat up with one finger. "He's a self-taught terror."

Helen grinned at him. "I'm afraid Mark is right. Clyde is very stubborn, and my aunt spoils him something fierce."

"Is he play motivated or is he food motivated?" the woman asked.

"He's mischief motivated," Mark answered.

Helen ignored him. "I'd say he is food motivated."

"Then you might try training him with some of these." She held out her baggie with a few remaining dog treats in it. "Bonnie will do just about anything for one."

Helen stood and took the bag from her. "What are they?"

"Peanut-butter flavored, all-natural, low-calorie dog snacks. I make them myself."

"Really? Clyde does enjoy peanut butter." She hadn't noticed before but many of the *Englisch* shoppers had their dogs with them.

Had that been the case at the Berlin market, or was this something that Apple Creek encouraged?

"I can write out the recipe, if you like. It's simple," the woman offered.

Helen smiled her thanks. "That would be very kind. I have a notepad and pencil."

The woman scribbled out the recipe and handed it to Helen. "I use a cookie cutter to make them bone-shaped, but small flattened balls will do just as well."

"*Danki*, thank you." Helen placed the notebook in her pocket, gave Bonnie one last pat on the head and walked off with Mark. Together, they strolled along the row of tents and booths until they came to a baker's display.

Mark took his time deciding on a cream horn while Helen chose a raspberry scone. They moved away to eat their purchases.

"Yours are better," he said after he popped the last bite in his mouth.

"These scones are *wunderbarr.*" Helen kept her eye on what people were buying from the baker as she nibbled. Although there were two beautifully decorated cakes in the display case, people were buying items that were easy to carry, and the baker was handing out order forms for special-occasion cakes to customers who expressed an interest. Packages of cookies, scones, cinnamon rolls and cake pops sold the best. Occasionally, someone bought a loaf of specialty bread.

"What do you see that you could incorporate into your booth next time?" Mark asked.

"Pretty tablecloths. I can easily invest in another table and an awning for shade. I wonder how much those acrylic display cases are."

"Why would you need them?"

She swatted at a fly buzzing around her face. "To keep the insects off the food. I'm going to ask the baker where he got them and how much they are."

She took a step toward the booth, but stopped and turned around. "Mark, I have to thank you. I don't know how long it would have taken me to figure this out by myself."

"You would have done it," he said, and she knew he meant it. The warmth that settled in her chest had little to do with his compliment and more to do with the admiration in his eyes.

Am I falling for him? I can't be. She turned away quickly. Their buggy ride home suddenly loomed large in her thoughts.

Chapter Ten

Only a few minutes into the trip home, Mark noticed that his talkative companion had grown strangely silent. "Is something the matter, Helen?"

Her bright smile looked forced. "Why should anything be the matter?"

"I don't know. You look worried."

"I was just thinking about everything I've learned today." She stared off into the distance.

"It might seem overwhelming now but if you break it down into small sections, you can implement the changes you need little by little."

She turned to look at him. "When did you become interested in how a business works? The Amish men I know want to farm as their fathers and grandfathers farmed and if they own a business, they want to run it as their father and grandfather did."

"You aren't giving us enough credit. We may look like we are farming as our grandfathers did with horses or mules, but we aren't. A lot has changed. Fertilizers and pesticides that our ancestors never dreamed about are now commonplace. Organic produce has become popular, so some farmers adapt and use the old ways to manage pests. Soil health is something that can be studied and improved. It's the same with any business. There are men who want to do a better job and improve their product even if it is the same product their grandfather sold. Unlike many *Englisch* businessmen, the Amish aren't in it to earn a lot of money. If we make enough to get by, that's our measure of success."

"Okay, but what inspired you?"

He glanced at her and saw she truly was interested. He wasn't used to talking about himself. "My father didn't own a farm. He was the oldest son. Isaac was the youngest, and he inherited grandfather's farm. Daed could have stayed and worked the farm with Isaac but he wanted his own business. He tried a number of different enterprises, and none of them worked out. After a while, he worked odd jobs for other people, but he was never content to stay in one place. Because of that, we moved around a lot."

"Rebecca told me that your mother died when you were young and that you came to stay with Isaac and Anna." Her sympathetic tone gave him the courage to share his story.

"I was eight. During the time I stayed with them, Isaac realized that farmland was becoming too expensive for all of his sons to eventually own their own land. He knew that to keep his family together he would have to have work that would provide a living for them. That's when he started his furniture-making business. Unlike my father, Isaac was able to grow and expand the business he started. Anna, too, had good business sense and opened her gift shop. By the time I was ten, I had realized that it wasn't chance or fate that made them successful. It was understanding how a business should be run."

"Perhaps it was because the Lord favored them."

One side of his mouth lifted in a half smile. "The Lord brings the rain and sun that makes your garden grow, but you must still pull the weeds if you want a good harvest."

"That was one of my grandmother's favorite sayings."

"It's one of Isaac's, too. That's why I came

to apprentice with him before I open my own furniture-making business. I have invested two years to learn all I can from him."

"And those two years are almost up. Where will you go after that?"

"Back to the village where my family lives in Pennsylvania. I have the land picked out where I will build my shop." He hoped that land was still available to him. He had not heard from Angela's father, and the uncertainty gnawed at him. Helping Helen gave him something to work toward and kept his mind busy.

He glanced her way. That wasn't the whole truth. Helping Helen made him feel good. Just being with her was somehow soothing and exciting at the same time. "Are you planning to stay in Bowmans Crossing?"

"I'm not sure. I have a good job, so I may stay. I'm fond of Charlotte even if she is a trial. Eventually, she will need someone to watch over her."

"You mean someone other than the dog?"

"Exactly. Clyde is already five years old, and his breed normally lives to be ten or twelve. When he's gone, I worry that Charlotte will have difficulty adjusting. She doesn't have any close family other than my parents and my sister in Indiana."

"The church will take care of her if need be."

"That's true. She has friends, too. I may be concerned about nothing."

"Isn't your goal to lead an independent life? I hope you know I respect that choice."

"I am leading my own life," she declared. "But sometimes plans change."

"Mine won't."

"What would you do if you couldn't purchase the land you wanted back home?"

"I won't think in terms of failure. I can't." He hoped Helen didn't notice the hint of fear that crept into his voice.

She laid a hand on his arm. "Then I pray God allows you to fulfill your dream."

Helen pulled her hand away and clasped her fingers tightly together. She didn't want Mark to think she was bold. Something in the sound of his voice told her how critical the success of his plan was to him. She sensed there was more to the story than a desire to start a business in Pennsylvania. Something about it was vitally important to him. Perhaps it involved the woman waiting for him back home. Maybe he didn't want to marry until he could support a wife and children. It made sense that Mark was that kind of man.

She remained silent for the rest of the ride

home. Mark didn't seem to notice, or at least he didn't comment. When they reached the workshop, he stopped beside her bicycle, and she got down. "*Danki*, Mark, I will carefully consider all the things you have told me."

"I hope I have helped."

"You have. I once thought you were arrogant and judgmental, but I was wrong. You have been both a good teacher and a friend. *Danki*."

He inclined his head. "I don't have many friends. I'm honored you count me as one of yours."

She watched him drive away, wishing there was some way she could pay him back for all he had done for her. Perhaps the day would come when she could.

Paul was standing just outside the front door of the building. Mark waved to him, and Paul waved back as he ambled toward Helen as she was getting on her bike. "My brother has been taking you up in his buggy often these days."

"He has been very kind to me considering what a problem Clyde has been." She didn't want to discuss her relationship with Mark.

Paul folded his arms over his chest and leaned one shoulder against the wall of the building. "I thought maybe I should tell you a few things about my brother. Things I figured you might not know. He doesn't like to talk about himself."

"I don't listen to gossip."

"It's not gossip. I love my brother, and I want him to be happy. I have a feeling you want the same thing."

She glanced at him and saw he was watching her intently. She hadn't given Paul enough credit. He was more than a jokester. "Your brother has told me quite a bit about himself."

He arched one eyebrow. "Now that is surprising. I don't want you getting your hopes up where he is concerned. He's a good catch, but he has an understanding with a girl in Pennsylvania."

"I know. My aunt told me that the first day I came here."

"I guess I didn't realize it was common knowledge."

"It is. I also know Mark is committed to running his own business someday."

"*Committed* is a good word. He doesn't compromise. He sets his mind to something and works until he has achieved it."

"Why are you telling me this?"

"I have the feeling that he likes you. Even admires you."

"I like and admire Mark, too. There's nothing wrong in that."

"Maybe not, but if you expect him to change his mind about his plans to return to fair Angela and his dreams back home, I'm here to tell you that you are wasting your time. Call it friendly advice, or call it a warning if you will. I like you, too. I don't want to see you get hurt, either."

"Then I thank you for your friendly advice, but it isn't needed. Mark and I are becoming friends, that's all. He's a good teacher, and I'm a willing pupil. Besides, I have plans of my own, and they don't include starting a romantic relationship with anyone, if that's what you're hinting at."

"It's good to know where you stand." He straightened, touched the brim of his hat and walked away.

Helen watched him go then got on her bike and pedaled for home. She had two uninterrupted miles to consider her feelings for Mark Bowman. By the time she reached her aunt's home, she had come to the decision that they might remain friends, but she would guard her heart against any deeper feelings. She wouldn't come between him and the woman named Angela.

During the rest of the week, Helen made

a point to avoid Mark as much as possible. When she couldn't, she maintained a friendly demeanor. She wondered if Paul had spoken to Mark about his concerns for the two of them. She had no way of knowing. She certainly couldn't bring herself to ask Mark outright.

With Mark's suggestions for her business in mind, she got ready for Friday's market. She asked Samuel to make her some wooden holders that would allow her to set her display trays at a slight angle for easier viewing. He offered her the loan of a canopy, which she gladly accepted. She had Jessica help her pay for her booth space online and order acrylic cases and domes from a bakeware website. The cases hadn't arrived by Thursday morning, and she resigned herself to doing without them for this week's market.

When Helen came home from work, she found Charlotte had spent the afternoon making a mountain of dog treats for Clyde from the recipe the *Englisch* woman with the bassett hound had given her. Clyde was snoring in the corner, and Helen wondered how many he had sampled.

To Helen's further surprise, Rebecca, Anna and Fannie showed up on Thursday evening to help her bake. Apparently, Mark had mentioned her project, and the women of the family were eager to see that Helen had a successful second day at the market. They were soon mixing, baking and sampling a variety of cupcakes, cake pops and even pie pops at Rebecca's suggestion. Rebecca donated a jar each of homemade peach, cherry and pumpkin pie filling. Charlotte happily joined in, but Helen noticed that she had trouble remembering how to seal the edges of the pie pops. Helen had to go back and reinforce all her efforts.

The kitchen was full of delicious aromas and cheerful chatter as the Bowman women regaled Helen with stories of their husbands and children. Good-natured teasing and a genuine interest in Helen's project soon had her feeling as if she had known these women for years. Surrounded by her new friends, Helen missed her mother and her sister even more. They would've enjoyed being part of the frolic. In spite of her sister's recent actions, Helen realized she had many fond memories of their times together while they were growing up. Perhaps she could forgive Olivia one day. Maybe she could forgive herself, too.

As the women were getting ready to leave that evening, Charlotte went out onto the porch and started calling for Juliet and clapping her hands. Charlotte turned to Helen, who had come outside with her. "I can't understand why Juliet is out so late this evening. She should've come in for supper before now."

Helen laid a hand on her aunt's arm. "Juliet has been missing for over a week now."

Charlotte looked puzzled for a few seconds then her gaze cleared. "That's right. How silly of me to forget that. I'm just so used to having her here with me."

She patted Helen's hand. "You and Mark are looking for her. Clyde certainly has taken a liking to you and to Mark. Dogs know things about people. I think I will go to bed now. I'm very tired. Come along, Clyde. Good night, all."

The dog trotted after her, his long brown ears occasionally getting in the way of his feet and causing him to stumble, although he didn't seem to mind. The dog hadn't made a single visit to his tree since the night Mark hit Helen in the eye with his slipper. Hopefully, the dog's nocturnal visits were done for good.

Helen followed Anna out to her buggy. "Does my aunt seem more confused to you?"

Anna shook her head. "Charlotte has always been a little scatterbrained. She's fine. I know she is happy to have you here."

"Really?"

"She was just telling me yesterday when

she stopped in for coffee what a blessing it has been having you stay with her."

"That's good to know. She has been a blessing to me, as well. I'm afraid I have been a self-centered person for much of my life. I didn't always consider how other people felt."

"We have seen none of that in you," Rebecca said from the front seat of the buggy.

"I hope I am improving. The good Lord has given me a lot to think about in these past weeks." Foremost among her thoughts was Mark and her growing feelings for him, but she didn't share that with anyone.

"Mark mentioned you wished to sell some of your baked goods in my store. Bring them by whenever it's convenient."

"Whatever I don't sell tomorrow I'll bring over." Helen waved goodbye to her company and went inside.

That night she sat down to pen a letter to her parents. She didn't want them to fret about her any longer. She had worried them enough.

After finishing her letter, she went to bed and tried to sleep, but her eyes wouldn't stay shut. She was too excited for the coming day. Would she earn enough money to make all her work worthwhile? Would she remember all that Mark had taught her? Would it rain?

She rolled over and hugged her pillow. She

was dying to know one certain thing. Would Mark be there again?

Mark sat up and glanced at the clock beside his bed. It was five thirty in the morning. He listened closely, but heard only the wind in the tree branches, the murmur of the river and the chirping of night insects. Clyde had failed to show again. Mark flopped back against his pillow with a big grin and stretched. Maybe the foolish dog was howling under someone else's window for a change, or maybe he was home sleeping as he should be.

Today was the day Helen was going to try selling at the farmers' market again. Mark was eager to see how much of his advice she took and how much her sales would improve because of it. He did want her to succeed.

Helen's resiliency in trying again so soon was admirable. He didn't know how she could shake off her humiliation so easily and get right back into the fray. She was a remarkable woman. Not at all like his first impression of her. Or his second. Or his third. He chuckled to himself at the memory of their meetings and her abject failures in her attempts to ask him for a job.

Helen Zook was persistent if nothing else.

She would succeed at her baking business or go down in smoke and flames trying.

After breakfast, Mark, Paul, Samuel and Isaac went down to the workshop. The rest of the crew soon arrived. Mark kept a lookout for Helen. The surge of happiness that hit him when he saw her took him by surprise.

His uncle handed Mark the clipboard with the daily announcements. Mark read them off and assigned men to each task. The last note on the page took some of the joy out of his day. He'd have to meet with clients this evening.

He looked at Helen. "We are expecting a shipment of lumber and assorted items later today. Helen, why don't you help Jessica in the office until they arrive. Samuel, I want you to make sure we get the right grade of wood. The company sent us a cheaper grade last time, and I had to send it back."

"What did you bring us to eat today, Helen?" one of the men asked. It was Adam Knepp, Isaac's master carver.

"A box of nails and wood chips," Jessica quipped.

Adam laughed. "Those gingersnaps the other day were as good as my Grosmammi Stutzman used to make."

Helen inclined her head. "*Danki*. It was

my grandmother's recipe. Maybe my grandmother and your grandmother knew each other. I didn't bring anything today as I am selling my goods at the market in Berlin this afternoon. You are welcome to come and *purchase* some of those gingersnaps."

Adam shook a finger at her. "I see what your plan is. You ply us with sweets until we expect them, and then you say, "Come buy them,' thinking we will spend our hard-earned money to enjoy your cooking."

Mark opened his mouth to defend her but before he spoke, she said, "Exactly. Is it working?"

"It is," Jessica said, and the men laughed. "My mom and I really enjoyed the oatmeal bread I bought from you last week. Can I buy it from you here?"

Helen smiled at Mark. "Anna says she has room for some of my baking in her gift shop. You should be able to get what you want over there. If you would care to give me your orders, I can make certain I fix what you like."

Several of the men crowded around her, listing items they wanted. Mark stepped in and raised his voice. "This can wait until break time. She isn't going home to make up a batch of cookies for you today. We have work to do."

As the men moved away to get started,

Helen remained beside Mark. "I didn't mean to be a distraction."

"I would be a poor boss if I couldn't get them to order baked goods on their own time. Are you ready for this afternoon?"

She nodded. "Anna, Rebecca and Fannie all came over to help me bake last night. I have nearly as much stuff to take as I did that first day."

He leaned close enough to smell the scent of fresh-baked bread that seemed to cling to her. "That must mean you have some confidence in my advice."

"I have a lot of confidence in the things you taught me, and I have baked things I think the market customers will enjoy." She looked down at her hands clasped in front of her. "Will you be going?"

"I wish I could, but don't count on me. I'm meeting with a couple of clients this evening who want to order a custom bedroom suite. I'm afraid I won't finish in time to stop by and see how you're doing."

She looked up at him with a sweet smile that warmed him clear through. "I have every intention of doing well, God willing. Is it all right if I make up some of my time tomorrow? Jessica has said she has filing I can do."

"That will be fine. I will be working on

that new mantelpiece for a while tomorrow. You can tell me all about your success or failure then."

"I refuse to think about failure." She spun around and went into the office.

Mark hadn't intended to work on the project but if she were going to be here, he would use it as an excuse to spend a little time with her. He liked Helen and enjoyed her company.

He realized he was still staring at the office door that she had vanished through. He spun around and got to work before anyone else noticed that he had a hard time taking his eyes off Helen Zook.

Charlotte arrived at the right time with the buggy Helen had loaded before she left that morning. The only thing Helen was upset to see was that she had Clyde with her. The dog woofed happily and wagged his tail. He tried to lick Helen's ear as she climbed in, but she managed to hold him off.

Mark came out of the building and waved to Charlotte before heading around to the lumber storage area. Charlotte turned to Helen. "Isn't Mark coming with us?"

"He has to meet with some customers."

"But he came last time."

"He didn't go with us. He went on his own."

Helen took the reins and soon had the horse trotting at a brisk pace on the road.

"Clyde would rather have Mark along." Charlotte looked behind them.

"Clyde and me both," Helen muttered.

The occasional car or pickup shot around them. One car passed them and then slowed down beside them in the oncoming-traffic lane so that a woman could lean out the car window and snap a picture with her phone. Helen turned her face aside and held up her hand. The car sped on. She turned to see Charlotte also had her hand in front of her face and was holding one of Clyde's ears over his face.

"They are gone, Aenti," Helen said, choking back a laugh. She couldn't wait to share the story with Mark.

Charlotte lowered her hand and dropped Clyde's ear. "Rude tourists. I have no idea why they feel the need to take pictures of us."

"They think we are quaint."

"Then they are silly, and they need to find better things to do."

"Let's hope they are on their way to the farmers' market and will buy our baked goods."

Helen was prepared to do whatever it took to make a profit this afternoon. More than anything, she wanted to prove to Mark that she could succeed. Tomorrow morning couldn't come soon enough.

Chapter Eleven

A loud howl followed by deep quick barks pushed aside Mark's pleasant dream and brought him to the edge of wakefulness. He stared at the dark ceiling, wondering if the sound might have been part of his dream. He closed his eyes and tried to slip back into sleep where Helen waited for him with a sweet smile on her lips and her arms out to welcome him.

The howl came again.

Not a dream.

"Unbelievable." Mark sat up.

He should have been annoyed, but he wasn't. Clyde's arrival meant Mark would get to spend an extra hour with the real Helen, not the confusing woman of his dreams who never let him close but who seemed ready to welcome him.

Knowing it wouldn't do any good to yell at Clyde, Mark got dressed, picked up his boots and went downstairs to open the back door. Clyde came padding in without being called. He woofed once and launched himself at Mark. Prepared for the impact, Mark managed to stay upright but had to drop his boots.

"Why can't you come calling at a decent hour, Clyde? This is so rude. And now I sound like Charlotte talking to a dog as if you can understand me."

Mark rubbed Clyde's big soft ears and then nudged him to the floor. Frisking like a puppy around Mark, Clyde followed him to the front door. Mark opened it and pointed to the road. "Go home."

Clyde flopped to the floor, put his head on his paws and whined.

"Is that a no?"

Clyde whined again.

"Want to go for a buggy ride?"

Bounding to his feet, Clyde wriggled eagerly. Mark rubbed the sleep from his eyes. "You know what 'go for a buggy ride' means, don't you? I sure wish you would learn 'go home.' It's almost time to get up anyway. Let me get my boots on."

He sat on a chair against the wall and smoothed his socks. Clyde came to smell his feet. The dog sneezed, making Mark laugh. "Can you keep a secret? I'm making a carved wooden spice rack for Helen. It was going to have solid doors, very Amish, very plain, but I have just now decided to decorate the doors with basset hound carvings. Do you think she'll like it?"

Clyde wiggled eagerly and woofed once.

"I think she will, too. Something to remember us by." He sobered as he considered the possibility that he might not see her again after he went home.

"Mark, who are you talking to?" Anna asked from the kitchen doorway.

"Charlotte's dog," he said without looking up.

She chuckled. "Is he answering you?"

"Not yet, but we are working on some sign language." He pulled on his left boot.

"Did you pick some of my tomatoes last night or this morning?"

"Nope. Clyde, are you stealing tomatoes now?"

The dog sat down and whined. Mark looked at his aunt. "I think that means no."

"Well, someone helped themselves to three big ripe ones I planned to pick this morning. Your breakfast will be waiting for you when you get back."

"Don't bother. I'm sure Helen has something to feed me."

"She is a *goot* cook, *ja*?"

"Not as fine as you but pretty close." He pulled on his right boot.

"Not married, pleasant, a baptized member of our faith and a *goot* cook. Charlotte even said she is glad Helen has come to visit. You could do worse."

He figured that he and Helen would become the subject of discussion after the church service tomorrow if he didn't put a stop to it. He stood and brushed his hands together. "She isn't looking for a husband. She wants an independent life. Her words, not mine."

"So, you have discussed this. That's a fine start."

He put his hands on his hips. "The start of what, Aenti Anna?"

"Courting."

"We aren't courting. We are simply friends. I'm taking her dog home to her. Again."

"And having breakfast there. Again. Tell Charlotte I said she has a very smart dog."

He shook his head at his aunt's nonsense and left the house with Clyde ambling behind him. At least he didn't have to drag the dog away anymore. After hitching up the buggy, he climbed in and Clyde scrambled up after him. The dog happily sat beside him during the ride and jumped out as soon as Mark pulled to a stop in front of Charlotte's house. He ran to the front door and started barking.

There was a light in the kitchen. Mark assumed someone was already up. A few seconds later, the door opened and Helen looked at the dog in amazement. "I don't believe it. How did you get out?"

She looked at Mark. "How is he getting out of this house?"

"My guess is that someone is letting him out."

Outrage filled her eyes. "Are you accusing me?"

He held up both hands. "I was thinking of your aunt."

Helen stepped aside so he could come in. "I can't believe she would willingly put him out in the middle of the night. She barely lets him out of her sight during the day."

He hung his hat on one of the pegs by the front door. "What's for breakfast?"

"I was about to make some oatmeal."

He made a face. "I was never very fond of it myself."

"I have some day-old croissants."

"Sounds great, if you have a cup of coffee to go with it." He sat down at the table.

She put her hands on her hips and glared at him. "I was just about to brew some. Make yourself at home, Mark Bowman. Don't mind me."

"I figured since I was already here, you would want to tell me all about your success at the market yesterday. Am I right?"

She raised one eyebrow. "What makes you think I was successful?"

He leaned back in his chair and grinned. "Because I taught you all that you needed to know."

"Oh, you did? How strange. I thought it was my hard work and my fine baked goods that won over the customers."

"So, you did have a successful day?"

"I did." She carried the coffeepot to the sink and filled it. "I sold eighty percent of the goods I took. The pumpkin pie pops were the biggest hit. I had several repeat customers throughout the afternoon for them and sold out before five."

"Where was your booth?"

"I had Jessica purchase it on the computer for me instead of waiting until I got there, so I was located near the middle of the grounds instead of down on the end."

"Good thinking. I'm sure a better location helped. How did the other bakery do?"

"Fair, I think. Several people commented that my bread prices were higher than his."

"And how did you respond to that?"

She giggled. "I told them the quality was higher, as well."

"Did they walk away?"

"They didn't, because I reduced my price to match his. It was near the end of the day, so I figured it was better than not making a sale. It was still within my profit margin for bread, so I didn't lose money on the loaves."

"You have the makings of a real business-woman, Helen. I'm impressed. Can you dupli-cate your success? That's the next question."

"I think I can, but you won't believe what brought in the most people."

"Had to be your cinnamon rolls." He wished she had saved him one.

She brought a plate with a croissant and several pieces of cheese and set it in front of him. "Nope, it was Clyde."

He slanted a glance at the dog sitting by his feet. "Clyde? Explain."

She added coffee grounds to the pot and put it on the stove before coming to sit at the table. "He was absolutely adorable. Charlotte sat out front of our booth on her chair, and he did trick after trick for her. Each time she gave him one of the treats she'd made, he'd sit up on his hind end and fall over with a smile of bliss on his face. I am not making this up."

Mark pointed to the hound at his feet. "This dog did tricks?"

"I'll show you." She went to the cupboard and took out a plastic bag full of small brown cookies. "Clyde, do you want a treat?"

He immediately woofed.

"Beg for one."

He sat back on his haunches, wobbling a little, and then waved his front legs together. She gave him a cookie. It disappeared in one gulp. Then he sank over sideways and rolled to his back. Mark had to admit he did look like he was smiling.

Helen was grinning from ear to ear. "Isn't he adorable?"

She was adorable. He realized he'd never seen her so happy. Her eyes sparkled with mirth. Her lips were parted in a sweet smile. Her excitement was infectious. He had trouble thinking about why he was here. "He's not adorable when he's barking outside our house in the wee hours of the morning."

Her grin faded. "You have a point."

Charlotte came into the kitchen from the hallway. "Helen, did you let Clyde out of my room? I can't find him. Oh, there he is," she said when she spied him. "Mark, how nice to see you. Have you come to give Helen a ride to work?"

"I've come to return your dog. He was howling outside my window again."

"How strange." Charlotte stared at Clyde. "What are you doing visiting the Bowmans at such an hour?"

He lay on his back, wagging his tail.

Helen passed out the coffee mugs and poured them all into a cup. "Are you sure you didn't open the door for him last night, Aenti?"

"I didn't open the front door, and I didn't open the back door for him. He must be getting out through my window."

Mark rose to his feet. "I'll take a look and secure it so he can't get out again."

Helen followed him down the hall. "I can't believe he can get out that way."

He opened the door to Charlotte's room. The window ledge was three feet off the floor and the sash was only up a few inches. There wasn't any furniture the dog could climb on near it. Mark was as baffled as Helen. "You're right. I don't see him getting out this way. I can cut a length of wood to act as a stop so he can't push the window open wider if he is getting up here."

They walked back to the kitchen where

Charlotte sat sipping her coffee. "Did you figure it out?"

"We didn't," Mark admitted. "I can build a kennel for him to stay in at night."

"Absolutely not." Charlotte plunked her coffee mug down. "I will not keep him in a kennel. He has been raised in this house. I wouldn't put either of you in a cage."

"Aenti, he can't keep waking up the Bowman family in the middle of the night. We have to be better neighbors."

Charlotte blinked back tears. "He would hate a kennel. If only Juliet would come home, he wouldn't be wandering around in the middle of the night looking for her."

The last thing Mark wanted was to make a woman cry. "I won't put him in a kennel."

She sniffed once. "You won't? I'm sure he won't get out again. I'll talk to him," Charlotte assured Mark.

Like that would help. He turned to Helen. "Are you ready to go to work?"

"Give me a minute to get my things together, and I'll be ready."

"I'll be in the buggy, waiting." He paused at the door and looked back. Charlotte had Clyde's face between her hands as she whispered something in his ear. He remembered what his aunt had said. "My aenti Anna says to tell you that you have a smart dog."

Charlotte looked at him. "She figured that out, did she? Anna was always a bright one."

Unsure of what she meant, he left the house and waited for Helen outside. It didn't take her long to join him. "Sorry to keep you waiting."

"That's okay. There isn't any rush. It will be just you and I at the workshop this morning."

"I'm glad you are letting me make up my lost hours. That's very kind of you."

"It's my *onkel's* rule. He doesn't want his workers to feel cheated. They have the opportunity for overtime work if they wish it."

"Will you have the same management style at your business?"

"Most likely. It may be a year or two before I can hire an extra worker, but I want to help support the community as my *onkel* is doing."

"That's a fine goal."

"It isn't about making money. It's about making a living for my family and others."

"You put me to shame."

"Why do you say that?"

"Because my only goal is to move out of my aunt's home before I tear my hair out."

"You would look odd bald. It's a worthwhile goal."

Helen regaled him with more stories of her day at the farmers' market. He listened to her with only a few comments, enjoying the sound of her voice and the undercurrent of excitement she couldn't contain. He couldn't remember the last time he had enjoyed a buggy ride so much.

When they finally reached the workshop, he got out and turned to help her. She rested her hands on his shoulders as he grasped her waist and swung her down. She was so close his mind stopped functioning. He couldn't release her, couldn't step away. Her upturned face was so close to his. All he had to do was lean forward a little and he could kiss her.

Helen held her breath as Mark's hands lingered on her waist. She gazed into his beautiful green eyes and wished with her whole heart that she could move closer. Her fingers rested lightly on his shoulders, and she could feel his firm muscles through the fabric of his white cotton shirt. She wanted to be kissed. And she had no right to wish such a thing. She looked down and stepped back. He released her and rubbed his hands up and down on his pant legs.

"What are you working on today?" she asked as she walked toward the workshop door.

"The people that I met with yesterday want a reproduction piece made to match the antique dresser that they have."

She couldn't be sure, but she thought his voice sounded strained. "I thought you were doing a mantelpiece."

"It can wait. These people are willing to pay a premium for a rush job."

"How soon do they want it?"

"Two weeks."

"Are you serious? Can you do it in two weeks?"

"If Samuel and I work on it together, we can."

Helen saw the antique dresser wrapped in plastic sitting in the middle of the work area. "This is what you have to copy?"

"That's it." He stopped beside it and began unwinding the protective sheeting.

"I shall leave you to it." She reluctantly walked away and entered the office. When Mark was being nice, he was a very attractive man. She liked him much more than she should. Keeping a guard on her heart wasn't as easy as she thought it would be.

An hour later, Helen had filed everything Jessica had set out for her. She cleaned and dusted the office area, including the shades on the windows, and mopped the floor. There was nothing left to fill her time, so she went out to find Mark. He was bent over a large drafting table where he was making a full-size, detailed drawing of the dresser. It sat beside him. He got up to measure the width and height of the legs. She didn't want to disturb him, so she turned to go.

"Leaving already?" He pulled his pencil from behind his ear and made a notation on the paper.

"I've done everything Jessica left for me. Unless you have some work that needs doing, I'm going to go home."

"Can you give me a hand with this for a few minutes?"

"Of course." She hurried to his side.

He held out his tape measure without looking up from his drawing. "Check to see that the drawer heights are the same on all three drawers. They don't look quite even."

"Sure." She took the tape measure, being careful not to touch him.

After checking and rechecking the drawers, she handed the tape back to him. "The bottom drawer is one-quarter inch shallower than the others." She read off the measurements, and he jotted them down.

He tapped his lips with the eraser end of his pencil as he stared into space. "I've been thinking."

"About what?"

"Clyde."

"I honestly don't know how to keep him in without putting him in a locked kennel or a dog crate, and I don't think Charlotte will stand for that."

"You are right about the window. I don't see how he can get out that way. Charlotte has to be letting him out."

"She is adamant that she isn't."

"I hate to call her a liar, but she must be." He spun around on his stool to look at her. "Maybe she sleepwalks. I have a little sister that does."

Helen shrugged. "I guess it's a possibility. How would we tell unless we saw her doing it?"

"I can't expect you to sit up every night all night."

"I'm the last person you want for that job. I can fall asleep at the drop of a hat."

"So you won't be any help."

"I could ask her if she sleepwalks. Your aunt might know. Some of her friends might know if she does, but I would hate to start a lot of speculation if I started asking questions. Charlotte is a very private person."

"We could ask Clyde. If he says no, then we don't have to ask anyone else."

"Ha-ha. Very funny."

"When the answer is no, he lays down on the floor and whines."

"Are you trying to tell me that you speak dog now?"

"Clyde and I are reaching an understanding." He wagged his eyebrows.

She looked down and giggled. "Be serious."

"Believe me, my sleep is serious business."

"I'm sorry he is making such a pest of himself.

"Me, too." He turned back to his drawing.

Helen hesitated. The desire to stay and watch him work was strong, but she forced herself to start toward the door.

"Helen, I have an idea."

She turned around to see a mischievous grin on his face. This was not the Mark she had met on the bus or even later. This fellow with his sparkling green eyes and infectious smile was downright dangerous for her heart. "Let's hear it. How do we find out how he is getting out without watching the house all night?"

"That's exactly what I intend to do. Would you care to join me in some detective work?"

"I should hear your entire plan before I agree, but *ja*, count me in."

After hashing over the details of their plan, Helen went home, and Mark went up to the house. The family was gathering for lunch. The men had come in from the fields and were taking their places at the table. The women were busy in the kitchen. Paul hopped up from his seat and waved an envelope at Mark. "Another letter for you."

"From Angela?" Had she changed her mind? Part of him wanted her to and yet part of him didn't want that.

"It's from her father." Paul handed it over.

Mark took it and stared at Otis Yoder's spidery script. Inside was the information Mark had been waiting for. Was the land still available, or had Angela's change of heart ruined all his years of planning?

Chapter Twelve

On Monday night, Helen waited until after midnight, then she quietly opened Charlotte's bedroom door and peeked inside. Clyde was snoring on his blanket in the corner. Her aunt was snoring, too. The curtain on the open window waved gently. The sash was up a foot. Enough for Clyde to squeeze through if he could get up there. Helen closed the door and liberally sprinkled flour on the wooden floor in front of it. She did the same outside the back door and outside the front door, then she slipped out of the house and crossed the yard to the buggy that was parked in the yard. She gave a squeak of surprise when Mark reached out to help her up.

"Shh." He held one finger to his lips.

"You frightened me. I wasn't expecting you to be here yet," she whispered as she climbed in. When Helen had finished with the buggy that morning, she'd left it positioned so that anyone in the driver's seat would have an unobstructed view of the front of the house and along the north side, where her aunt had her bedroom.

"Did you put fresh flour on the outside of the doors like I told you?"

She nodded and then realized he couldn't see that in the dark. "I did just as you suggested. I also put some in front of my aunt's bedroom door. Anyone who goes that way will leave footprints. He has to be getting out her window somehow, but for the life of me I can't see how he is getting up to it. There's nothing under it that he can climb up on. Even standing on his hind legs, he can barely reach the window ledge with his front feet. I'm beginning to think he flies up by flapping those long ears."

"Now you're just being ridiculous."

"What's ridiculous is sitting in front of my aunt's house in the dead of night spying on a dog."

"You can go back in if you want."

"And miss the sight of Clyde flying out an open window? No way."

"He doesn't usually show up at my place until three or four in the morning. That means we may have a long wait ahead of us. Some nights he doesn't come in all. Are you sure you are up to this?"

"I'm as eager to solve this riddle as you are." But was she? Having Mark arrive with Clyde in time for breakfast and then drive her to work was something she enjoyed, but she could hardly admit that to Mark.

"I suggest that we take turns watching while the other one gets some rest. I can take the first watch."

"That's very practical, but I'm not the least bit sleepy at the moment. Why don't I take the first watch?"

"Okay." He scooted down to rest his head against the seat back and folded his arms across his chest.

His wide shoulders took up so much room that Helen had to scoot over to put a little distance between them so that their arms and shoulders weren't touching. She soon realized that not touching him didn't help. His presence beside her in the dark left her nerves standing on end. She scooted farther away, but that made the door handle poke her hip. She huffed and scooted back an inch.

He lifted his hat from over his face. "Is something wrong?"

"*Nee*, I'm just trying to get comfortable."

"It's hard to sleep with you bouncing up and down on the seat."

"I'm not bouncing up and down," she snapped.

"It feels like it to me."

She rolled her eyes. "I'm sorry. I'll try to be still."

He lowered his hat over his face. *"Goot."*

Helen stuck her tongue out at him and then had to stifle a giggle. She couldn't remember the last time she'd been that childish or enjoyed such excitement.

"What's so funny?" he asked without looking.

"Nothing," she said quickly and folded her hands primly in her lap. If Mark wasn't uncomfortable with their close proximity, then she wouldn't be, either. She focused her attention on the silent house. A three-quarter moon rose behind her and cast long black shadows in the gray darkness. The slow progress of the moon across the night sky was the only way to tell the passage of time.

Twice, she jerked herself upright after starting to doze off. Finally, she gave in and shook Mark's arm. He sat up. "Did you see something?"

"Nothing but the inside of my eyelids. It's your turn to keep watch."

He leaned forward to look up at the night sky. "It must be after two. Get some sleep, if you can. I'll wake you if I see a dog gliding out the window with his ears outstretched."

"Please do." Now that Mark was awake, Helen realized she was no longer sleepy. She sat silent for a few minutes then leaned toward him. "Have you ever done anything like this before?"

"Nope."

"Me neither."

"I find it hard to believe that a woman desirous of an independent life hasn't done a little sneaking around after dark."

"I did my share of running around with my friends as most Amish teens do during their *rumspringa*."

"And where did the scandalous Helen Zook go?"

"To the movies. Twice, no, three times. I went to five or six barn parties, but I didn't care for the loud music and dancing the kids were doing. Where did you go when you sneaked away from home?"

"I never did."

She turned to face him. Her eyes had adjusted to the dark. "Are you serious? You never slipped out to attend a movie or a barn dance or to have your *Englisch* friends drive you to a party?"

"Nope."

"I never figured you for a square."

"I was the oldest in the family. I had a responsibility to be a role model for the younger ones."

"Your responsibility is something you take seriously, isn't it?"

"Absolutely."

"I wasn't so *goot*."

"Why doesn't that surprise me?"

She heard the humor in his voice and knew he was teasing. "I never did anything I was ashamed of back then. I gave it all up when I took my baptismal vows. Have you taken yours?"

"I have. Three years ago."

"Because you intended to marry the girl back home?"

He shook his head. "We didn't have an understanding then. I knew I was going to remain Amish and saw no reason to delay."

"Was there anything that you hated to give up?" She tried to imagine the stern young man he would have been. In truth, he probably wasn't a lot different from the way he was now.

"I didn't like giving up my education. I got

permission from our bishop to attend business night classes at a local high school. The teacher there took an interest in me and did some private tutoring. She made sure I expanded my vocabulary. After that, I read extensively. I still do. I don't feel there is anything crucial that I have missed by being Amish. Being close to God is worth any sacrifice. What do you miss? Parties?"

"I had a cell phone," she admitted wistfully. "Four of my friends had them, too. We talked all the time."

"Do you miss your friends back in Indiana?"

"I miss them and my family. I was close to my mother and father."

"You aren't close anymore?"

"They took my sister's side. I was bitterly disappointed that they did. Rebecca told me a little about your family. It sounds as if your father disappointed you, too."

He was silent for so long that Helen thought he wasn't going to discuss it, but eventually he cleared his throat and said, "More than once."

Mark couldn't believe he was sharing that part of his life with Helen. Somehow, sitting in the dark made it easier to talk. He couldn't see the sympathy in her eyes, but he knew it was there. She cared about him as he cared about her. The tenderness she evoked in him was unlike anything he'd ever known. Was it possible he was falling for her? He pushed the thought aside and refused to examine it.

"Some people say talking about your troubles helps," she said softly.

"Some people are wrong," he quoted her own words back to her.

"A few of them are right. In what way did your father disappoint you?"

"It's ancient history. You don't want to hear it."

"Mark, you and I have become friends. You have helped me so much. I won't judge you or your family. If you want to talk, I'll listen."

He did want her to know, and that surprised him. "It's no dark secret. Many know my father is a failure in just about every sense of the word. He never could hold a job. He couldn't take care of my mother when she became ill. I was sent to live with anyone who said I could stay with them. Most people were very kind. A few were not. They saw me as an unpaid laborer, and I had to work very hard. Every time Daed dropped me off with a new friend or relative, I didn't know if he would come back for me. He'd be gone for months without sending any word. Then one day he would show up, and we'd be together for a few weeks before I was sent away again."

"That must have been terrible for a small child."

It soothed his soul that she understood. "Fortunately, when I was eight, he sent me to live with Isaac and Anna. That was the best thing that ever happened to me. I became a part of a real family. I saw how a mother and father could work together to provide for their children. I saw carefully laid plans brought to fruition by hard work."

"But you eventually went back to live with your father."

"He met and married a fine woman. The day I met my new mother, I met my new brother, Paul. We hit it off and became best friends. I have five younger sisters now, too, but it was years before I got over the fear that my father would send me away again. He still bounces from job to job, but Mamm has put her foot down. She won't move. Paul and I send money home for her and the girls. Daed is the reason I've got to make a success of my business back home."

"Are you hoping to impress him or prove that you can do what he never could?"

He shook his head. "You have it all wrong. If I am running a successful business, he will always have a job with me no matter how often he quits and comes back. Best of all, I will be living and working a short walk down the road from my family. My sisters will never have to worry about being split up and sent away if something should happen to their mother."

Helen leaned in and kissed his cheek. "Thank you for sharing this with me."

He froze in astonishment, glad she couldn't see how red his face must be turning.

She sat back. "You are a much better person than I am."

"I find that hard to believe."

"You wouldn't if you knew more about me."

He cleared his throat. "I told you about my past and my plans. Turnabout is fair play."

"I'm serious. I wasn't a nice person. I don't want to lower your opinion of me."

He wanted her to trust him enough to confide in him. "My opinion of you has gone from pretty low to fairly high in the space of two short weeks. I accept who you are now. Not who you were before. But if you don't wish to tell me, I understand."

Helen hesitated. Not because she didn't believe him but because she didn't like to remember the hurt she had caused. He waited patiently without saying anything else, so she asked God for strength and started speaking. "Do you remember me telling you that my fiancé announced he wanted to marry my sister a few weeks before our wedding?"

"I remember."

"That isn't the whole story. Joseph was considered an excellent catch in our community. His grandfather is our bishop. His father owns a prosperous farm, and Joseph was his only son." She wished she could gloss over the rest, but it was time to admit that she had been at fault, too.

"My friends and I were all smitten with Joseph. We were shocked when he bypassed us and asked my sister, Olivia, to walk out with him. Olivia is gentle and quiet. She's never said a bad word against anyone. She works hard and never complains, but she isn't the brightest person. She didn't do well in school."

"School grades don't determine a person's success in life."

"I know, but it was humiliating that my little sister was going out with the most eligible man in our district. I set out to take him away from her. I was coy, I used flattery, I put it into my sister's head that he really liked me and was just being kind to her. She believed me and stopped going out with him. I consoled him after telling him she wasn't in love with him. I made sure I saw him often. One day, he asked to walk out with me."

"That doesn't seem like the Helen Zook I know."

"The Lord has taken me down a peg or two since that time, and I deserved it. Eventually, Joseph proposed to me, and I had everything I desired. Then his mother became ill. Olivia went to help care for her. In the weeks that she worked for his family, Joseph rediscovered what a treasure Olivia is. He asked me to release him from his promise. I said no. Eventually, he got up the courage to take matters into his own hands. He told my parents and his grandfather, the bishop, that he could not in good conscience marry me."

"It was for the best."

"I know that now but I didn't then. Word of my humiliation spread quickly. The morning of their wedding, I decided to leave. I never told anyone where I was going. I wasn't sure Charlotte would take me in. When she heard my version of the story, she wasn't as sympathetic as I expected, but she let me stay for the summer."

"So you weren't in love with Joseph?"

"That's the irony of it. I grew to care a great deal for Joseph, and I prayed he would one day love me half as much as he loved my sister. The tears you saw me weeping on the bus were real. I was selfish and cruel, and I didn't deserve his love. I hurt two kind and gentle people with my false pride. I ran away rather than face what I had done. I left them to worry and wonder where I was rather than offering them the blessings they deserve. I did find the courage to write my parents and tell them where I'm staying. They haven't written back yet. So now you know."

"I don't think any less of you for hearing this story. You have recognized your flaws, and you seek to overcome them. You have shown compassion to Charlotte. I've seen you work hard at your job and at your baking business. I'm pleased to call you my friend."

Mark was more understanding than she deserved. Her attempts to keep her feelings for him those of a friend were quickly coming undone. "Angela is a blessed woman," she whispered.

He looked away. "Angela has had a change of heart. She has ended our understanding."

"What? How could she? Why would she?" Helen's voice rose. He hushed her with a finger to his lips.

"Did she say why?" Helen whispered.

"She didn't give a reason in her letter to me.

I heard from her father yesterday. He wrote to say she has not given him a reason, either. Only that she believes she made a mistake in agreeing in the first place. He says he will continue to try to persuade her to honor her agreement, but he considers I am at fault, too, for staying away and not securing her affections after all this time. He also says he will not sell me the land I need unless we are wed."

"You should go home and find out what's wrong. As a friend and as a woman, I'm telling you that you need to speak to Angela in person."

It wasn't the reaction he expected from Helen, but he wasn't sure what he thought she would say. "I will give some thought to your suggestion. It seems pointless to spend the money to travel now when I return for good in another month."

"You shouldn't delay."

Was she right? Without the property he wanted or the money he had paid to Angela, he had no option left but to start over from scratch. His well-thought-out plans had come to nothing. He was at fault. He saw that now. He had neglected to consider Angela's needs in their arrangement, but rushing back to her wasn't the answer. Even if she changed her mind, he couldn't enter into a loveless marriage. It wasn't Angela he wanted by his side for the rest of his life. It was Helen.

Movement on the north side of the house caught his attention. Glad for the distraction, he sat up straight. "Something is going on."

"Can you see what?"

It was hard to distinguish things in the patchwork of shadows cast by the moon. "It looks like your aunt is sticking something out of her window."

"I think you're right. Is that a board?"

They watched in silence as Charlotte pushed a long plank out her window and let the end drop onto the grass. Mark realized what she was doing. "It's a ramp."

The words were no sooner out of his mouth than Clyde scrambled out the window and trotted down the plank. He took off at a run toward the Bowman house. Helen looked at Mark. "She lied to my face."

"Technically, she didn't. She said she did not open the front door or the back door for him."

Helen scrambled out of the buggy. "She lied by omission, and she has a lot of explaining to do."

"You talk to her. I'm going to try and intercept Clyde before he wakes the household."

"Take my bike."

"*Danki*, but my horse and buggy are just down the road."

Helen entered the house and went straight into her aunt's bedroom without knocking. Charlotte was pulling the outside board in through the wide-open window. An identical board led from the window to the floor. Clyde had merely trotted up, over and out.

"Aenti, what do you think you are doing?"

Charlotte spun around with the slats in her hands. She crossed the room and slipped them under her mattress. "I'm making my bed dear. Is there something you need?" She tucked the sheet in and turned to face Helen.

"I need an explanation. Mark and I saw you let Clyde out the window."

Charlotte clasped her hands behind her back. "You did?"

"Why would you want to annoy the Bowmans like this?"

"Oh, I'm not trying to annoy the Bowmans. Anna is a good friend of mine. Clyde wanted to make sure Mark had an opportunity to spend time with you."

"Don't put any of this on Clyde. He's a dog. You, on the other hand, know better.

Poor Mark has missed hours of sleep because of you."

"I'm trying to tell you it wasn't entirely my idea. Clyde likes Mark and you, too. He thinks the two of you belong together. I've merely been helping Clyde achieve his goal. He fancies himself something of a matchmaker."

"I don't care what Clyde thinks. Mark and I are friends, and that's all. He is leaving in a few weeks, and I will probably never see him again." The words tightened Helen's throat. She was going to miss him. She hadn't realized how much until this moment.

"How do you get him to go to the Bowman house every time he is loose?" Helen still couldn't believe her aunt had concocted such a scheme.

"I don't tell him where to go. I believe he is looking for Juliet, and I don't understand why he insists on stopping at the Bowman's tree unless it's to summon Mark."

"I'm ashamed of you, Aenti Charlotte. I don't know how I'm going to explain your far-fetched scheme to Mark without dying of embarrassment. A matchmaking dog. That's just ridiculous."

"Please don't tell that to Clyde. You'll hurt his feelings."

Helen shook her head in disbelief. She

forced herself to use a milder tone. "Go to bed and get some sleep. I'll wait up for Mark to bring Clyde home."

"Are you angry with me?" Charlotte looked ready to cry.

"We'll talk about this in the morning."

Helen went to the kitchen and put the coffeepot on the stove. She wanted a freshly brewed pot ready when Mark returned. She had a feeling they might need it.

A half hour later, she heard the buggy pull up outside and went to open the door. Clyde came galloping in with his ears streaming back. He slid to a halt at her feet and looked up with a happy expression.

Mark's expression wasn't quite so happy. "What did she have to say?"

"It's all Clyde's doing. He fancies himself a matchmaker, and he gets you up so you can come spend time with me."

"She said that?" He rubbed a hand through his hair as he blew out a deep breath.

"She did and with a straight face. What am I going to do with her? I'm worried something is seriously wrong. Should I take her to see a doctor?"

"I don't know what to tell you. Maybe you should speak to Anna or Rebecca. Rebecca has nursing experience."

"Charlotte owes you and your family an apology if nothing else, but I will seek Anna's council. She has known Charlotte a long time. Do you want some coffee?"

"Sure."

Helen needed to do something. Mark moved to stand beside her. She pulled down the cups and started to hand him one but dropped it. They both tried to catch it, but it hit the floor and broke. Helen stared at the shattered pieces. "Do you think my unexpected arrival put too much stress on Charlotte's mind, or is Juliet's disappearance to blame?"

"Your aunt told Anna that she enjoys having you here. Maybe the loss of Juliet was too much."

Tears stung Helen's eyes and closed her throat, making it hard to speak. "I wish I knew what to do."

Mark drew her into a hug. "We'll figure it out. She'll get all the care she needs."

Helen rested in his arms with her head tucked beneath his chin. She'd never felt more comforted than she did at that moment. "I don't want to hurt one more person with my selfishness."

"You aren't." He slipped his hand under her chin and tipped her face up to meet his gaze. "You need to be strong for her."

"I don't feel strong."

"But you are. God placed you with Charlotte for a reason, and I think it was because she was going to need someone special."

"I'm not special."

He leaned close and rested his forehead against hers. "I think you are," he whispered.

His arms tightened around her. She knew he was going to kiss her.

Chapter Thirteen

Helen's lips were a breath away from his. Mark wasn't sure how they had gotten so close to his, but the desire to kiss her was a great weight pressing him closer still. It took every ounce of strength he had to hold himself that breath away.

He had nothing to offer her. Not even a plan for the future. How could he begin courting her when she thought he should go back to Angela? Rather than fight a losing battle, he moved slightly to the side and kissed her cheek. The softness of her skin beneath his lips startled him and begged him to explore the contours of her face. She turned away, leaving him bereft in a swirling sea of confusion.

It wasn't friendship or a wish to comfort

her that quickened his pulse and robbed the air from his lungs.

He didn't understand the powerful attraction she held for him, but he was starting to believe it was love. He stepped back and let his arms fall to his sides. With a little more distance between them, he was able to think coherently. "It's late. I should be getting home."

She knelt and began picking up the broken pieces of the cup. "Please tell Anna and Rebecca that Charlotte and I will come by for a visit later this morning."

"I will." Should he apologize for kissing her? Maybe it was better to pretend the gesture was meant to comfort her. If she didn't say anything, he wouldn't, either.

"I won't be into work. I don't think Charlotte should be left alone. I hope you understand." She didn't look at him.

"Jessica can take care of anything that comes along. Let me know if you need something."

"I'm okay. We'll be okay. Clyde can sleep in my room for the rest of the night. You don't need to worry about a return visit."

"I was just getting used to him as my alarm clock."

She didn't smile as he hoped she would. She still hadn't looked at him. Rising to her feet, she carried the debris to the wastebasket and dropped it in. "*Danki*, Mark, for everything."

"I'll see you later. Get some rest now, and try not to worry about Charlotte."

She finally glanced his way and managed a shaky smile. "I'll do my best. Good night."

"Guten nacht."

The urge to take her back in his arms sent him out the door, wishing he wasn't quite so strong but thankful that he'd come to his senses in time. How would he avoid giving in to the temptation to kiss her when he saw her every day? As he climbed into his buggy, he realized the answer was simple. He couldn't be alone with her. Or he had to convince her that she was the woman he wanted to court.

Everything he thought he knew about love had changed in the last few days. It wasn't a frivolous feeling. It was a deep and profound emotion that made his heart ache with the need to be close to Helen. He'd never be the same after tonight. He'd never look at her the same way again.

What was he going to do about it?

He had no idea how she felt about him beyond her friendship, but she professed to want an independent life, not marriage. Could he change her mind? Should he try, or would that destroy the very real friendship they shared? He wasn't sure what to do.

He had to have a plan.

Thunder rumbled in the distance as a sprinkle of rain began falling. He watched the light in the kitchen window until it grew dim and faded. The glow soon brightened the window near the back of the house, and he knew she had gone down the hall to her bedroom.

The wind rose, and the rain began in earnest, hitting the top of his buggy as the storm rolled in. He waited until Helen's light went out before he started for home. He had a lot of thinking to do and new plans to make. He'd never courted a woman before, but he intended to court Helen Zook. And he was going to need help.

Charlotte was as cheerful as ever the next morning when Helen entered the kitchen. She was scrambling eggs. "I made some coffee, if you want it. What would you like to take for your lunch today? We have some leftover meatloaf that would make a good sandwich."

"I'm not going to work today, so you don't need to make my lunch. I thought we should visit Anna today. You owe her and Isaac an apology."

"I guess I do, but Anna will understand.

She knows about Clyde's talent." She carried the skillet to Clyde's bowl and gave him a portion of eggs before moving to the table and dividing the rest between her plate and Helen's. The two women ate in silence. Helen was glad for that. She couldn't make idle chitchat if she wanted to.

She had been sure that Mark intended to kiss her. Why had he given her a peck on the cheek instead? Had she mistaken his intentions? Had the bold way she offered her lips to him disgusted him? It would be difficult to pretend she cared about him as a friend when he was so much more. The sensible thing was to avoid being alone with him in the future.

"What did you and Mark talk about for so long last night?" Charlotte asked, looking at Helen over the rim of her coffee cup.

"This and that. Nothing really. Chitchat mostly."

"Strange. I was certain I heard you talking about me."

Helen leveled a stern look at Charlotte. "Were you eavesdropping?"

Charlotte shook her head. "Absolutely not. I just happen to be in the hallway outside the kitchen doorway."

"Why were you in the hallway?"

"That's a silly question. I couldn't hear a thing in my room." She winked at Helen.

Helen had to smile at her confession. "Eavesdroppers rarely hear anything good about themselves."

"*They* say that's true, but I still don't know who *they* are. What time are we going over to see Anna?"

"After I do these dishes and wash a load of clothes. I don't have a single clean apron to wear. Everything is covered in flour."

"You will have to invest in some material to make more white ones. Flour won't show on them as much. I will go fill the washer for you. I think we are done with the rain, so you can hang them out on the line without a worry."

It took about Helen an hour and a half to wash her aprons and dresses along with several of Charlotte's in the surprisingly new wringer washer Charlotte had on her back porch. When the line of blue and mauve dresses and black aprons were fluttering on the clothesline at the side of the house, Helen hitched up the buggy and waited for her aunt to join her. She came out a few minutes later with Clyde trotting beside her.

It didn't take long to reach the Bowman house. Paul was outside and offered to take care of the horse, and the two women went in.

Anna greeted each of them with a holy kiss on the lips, surprising Helen. The gesture was normally used at baptisms in Helen's congregation. It wasn't common practice to do it outside of a special occasion.

"Come in the living room and sit down," Anna said. "Rebecca and Lillian are here, too."

"Where is Mark?" Charlotte asked, taking a seat.

"He and Isaac are trying to decide the best way to take that old tree down. A limb broke off and hit the roof in the storm last night. I'm sure he'll be in soon." Anna took a seat beside Charlotte.

The silence stretched for an uncomfortable long minute until Charlotte turned to Helen. "Aren't you going to tell them how crazy I am?"

"You aren't crazy, Aenti," Helen rushed to reassure her. "But you have put this family through some uncomfortable nights by your actions. You need to apologize."

Charlotte chuckled and smiled at Anna. "Clyde has been matchmaking again."

"So I have noticed," Anna replied with a grin. She patted the dog sitting beside her.

Charlotte cast a sidelong glance at Helen. "My niece doesn't believe he has such a talent."

"Dogs can't be matchmakers. It's not possible," Mark said from the doorway. He entered the room and sat down across from Helen. She was glad to have him there.

"Actually, Clyde has something of a reputation for doing just that," Rebecca said gently.

Helen couldn't believe what she was hearing. "You can't be serious."

"Oh, she is," Lillian added. "I've seen it myself."

"You met Grace Yoder at the frolic, didn't you?" Charlotte asked.

Helen combed her memory. "The elderly lady in the wheelchair?"

Charlotte nodded and leaned forward in her chair. "Last year she was attending a wedding for one of our nice young couples. She was Grace Troyer then. I needed my hands free, so she offered to hold Clyde's leash. She tied it to the arm of her wheelchair. Clyde bolted across the lawn, pulling her behind him, and ran right into Silas Yoder. He ended up in Grace's lap as Clyde raced down the lane, pulling both of them. When he stopped and people caught up with them, Grace and Silas were sharing a great laugh. She said it was the most fun she had had in years. It wasn't two months before their banns were announced. Everyone was stunned except Clyde and me."

"It was a coincidence," Mark said with a dismissive gesture.

Rebecca gave a slight shake of her head. "We can name four other instances where Clyde's activities brought couples together who wouldn't normally have gone out with each other. They all married."

Helen rose to her feet and paced across the room and back. "This is ridiculous. Mark and I aren't meant to be a match."

"Clyde thinks so," Charlotte declared. "I might be a little crazy, but I usually understand what my boy is telling me."

Mark rose to his feet. "This is food for thought."

Helen spun to face him. "You can't be serious."

He headed for the door but paused to look back. "I have work to do. Since Charlotte is fine, perhaps you could come out to the shop and give us a hand, Helen?"

She caught the slight come-with-me nod he gave her as he opened the door. It was better than staying and listening to this nonsense. Besides, she wanted to hear his explanation of food for thought.

His aunt spoke up. "Helen, I wanted to ask you before you go if you would be able to work in the gift shop for a few hours a week from Wednesday? The family has been invited to a picnic with Fannie's family. It's her birthday, but I hate to close the shop. We have an Amish country tour bus scheduled to stop for refreshments that day."

Charlotte huffed and crossed her arms. "Tourists. There are more every day."

"They are *goot* for business, and we must show kindness to strangers," Anna said with a stern look for Charlotte, who rolled her eyes without commenting.

"I'd be happy to help out," Helen said, eager to be gone.

Anna smiled. "*Danki*, my dear."

"We'll see that Charlotte and Clyde get home later this morning," Lillian added.

Helen went out the door with Mark, forgetting for the moment that she wasn't going to be alone with him anymore. Once they were away from the house, she hurried to keep up with him. "You don't believe any of that, do you?"

He kept walking. "That a dog knows who should marry? Of course not. But Charlotte believes it, so we will play along to keep her happy, and she'll keep Clyde at home."

Helen stopped. "What do you mean play along?"

He turned to face her and hooked his

thumbs under his suspenders. "We do what we've been doing. I'll come by for breakfast and give you a ride to work. I'll even go to the market with you. The difference will be that I, and the whole house, can sleep until a decent hour."

"I'm not sure about this." Wasn't spending time with him what she wanted to avoid?

"Let's give it a try. If it doesn't work out, we'll try something else."

"Okay. I guess I can do that for the few weeks you have left here." She tugged nervously on the ribbons of her *kapp*. She could pretend they were still friends for that long, couldn't she?

Mark almost shouted for joy when she agreed. He never would have believed his courting help would come from a dog. God had a wondrous sense of humor. Mark didn't have a new plan for his business yet, but he was willing to give the problem over to God to solve for the first time in his life. A great weight lifted from his shoulders.

Inside the woodworking shop, Mark began carving the intricate detail along the edge of the reproduction dresser while Helen went to work in the office.

An hour later, Mark looked up to see his

uncle watching him. He straightened. "Is there something you wanted?"

"I just like to watch a fine craftsman at work." He moved closer and drew his hands around the surface. "This is *goot* work, Mark. You are getting better all the time."

Mark took a step back. "I like to bring the beauty God put into the wood out for all to see."

"The understanding and respect you have for the piece shows. If you weren't so set on your own plan, I'd tell you to follow your heart and see where it leads you."

Mark frowned at his uncle. "I don't know what you mean."

Isaac laid his hand on Mark's shoulder. "You have a head for business, but you have the heart of an artist."

Isaac left the work area, leaving Mark to stare after him and ponder his words.

It wasn't until later in the afternoon that Helen left the office. He saw her coming his way and slipped her nearly complete spice rack beneath his table.

She turned her head first one way and then another to study the dresser top he had finished. "That's *goot*, Mark."

"I'm satisfied."

The smile she pasted on her face looked as

if it might crack. "Have you decided what you are going to do about Angela?"

He took a deep breath. "I'm not going home to see her."

"Then you should write her a letter and explain how you feel," Helen stated firmly.

"She doesn't want to marry me."

Helen kept her gazed fixed on the dresser, avoiding his eyes. "You haven't even tried to change her mind. Have you told her you miss her and how much you look forward to the end of your time here? If you haven't said it in so many words, she doesn't know those things. A woman needs to know how a man truly feels about her in plain words. You can't leave her guessing."

What did Helen want to hear from a man who was falling in love with her? Who better to tell him than her? "What could I write that would change a woman's mind? What would you want to hear?"

Helen stared down at his tabletop. "We aren't talking about me."

He picked up a pen and took a clean sheet of paper from his top drawer. "Where do I start? *Dear* or *dearest*?"

She looked at him. "How do you usually start your letters?"

"I just use her name. 'To Angela, my sister in Christ.'"

"Then I would start with *my dearest Angela*."

"*My dearest*. All right, what else could I say that might win her over?"

Helen straightened the tools on his desk and lined them up neatly. "Tell her what is in your heart."

"Like what?"

"How do you feel when she isn't with you?"

He bent over the paper. "Every day that I am not with you is like living inside a dark cloud. How is that?"

"Nice."

"Just nice?"

"You can do better."

"You bring light to my world, to my heart and soul. My heart smiles every time I close my eyes and imagine your face. I dream that one day your heart will smile back at mine."

"That's beautiful, Mark."

"You like it?"

Helen cleared her throat. "I'm sure she will."

He bent over his paper again. "When I can't sleep, I look up at the moon in the night sky, and I wonder if you are looking at it, too. It comforts me to know you and I share something so lovely." He looked up. "What else should I say?"

"Tell her what she does that makes you happy"

"Everything you do makes me happy."

"Specifics are better."

He nodded. "I love the way you tap your foot when you are feeling impatient, and that cute pout on your lips makes me want to kiss you into a better mood."

Helen stepped back and put her hands in her pockets. "You have the idea now. No point in my eavesdropping any longer."

"Would those words make you come back to a man?"

She gazed at him. "Only if I knew that he loved me."

"How could you be sure of that?"

"By the way he kissed me." She looked away. "Go see her in person."

"Did you know Joseph didn't love you by the way he kissed you?"

"Maybe I did." She marched out of the room, letting the door slam behind her.

Mark sighed. How could he convince Helen of his feelings if she thought he wanted a different woman? How could he make her believe the truth?

He turned back to his work and noticed

Paul standing a few feet away. How much had he overheard?

"I wondered what was wrong with you. Now I know," Paul said, coming to stand beside Mark.

"What do you think you know?"

"You're in love with Helen. *The moon in the night sky*, I may use that line myself."

"Helen was helping me write a letter to Angela."

"That's not who you were thinking of. I saw your face when you looked at Helen."

"Okay, I wasn't writing to Angela. I was trying to find out what Helen would want to hear from a man who's falling in love with her."

"Want some advice?"

"No. Yes." Mark raked both hands through his hair. "I had everything figured out, Paul. I had a way to build a business with Angela's father that would keep Daed working and provide security for our sisters so they would never have to be sent to live with strangers."

"Whoa." Paul leaned in to look Mark in the eyes. "Why would our sisters ever be sent to live with strangers?"

Mark shrugged. "Bad things happen."

"Like your mother dying?"

"That's right. And like your father."

Paul took Mark by his shoulders and gave him a gentle shake. "I know your dad shuffled you off to different places when he couldn't get work. Mamm told me about that, but you and I would never let that happen to our sisters. Would we?"

Paul slapped a hand to his chest. "I wouldn't let that happen. We are a family. We'll always be a family, and we'll always look out for each other. Isaac and Anna, Noah and Fannie, Samuel and Rebecca and their children, Timothy and Lillian, Joshua, Mary and Hannah, Luke and Emma, my mother and all our sisters and your father and the members of our church, not to mention our God in heaven who looks after all His children. You aren't alone, Mark. You aren't the only one responsible for what happens to us."

Mark wrestled with his need to be in control even as he realized how fruitless his attempt had been. "But I'm the oldest son."

Paul straightened. "You might be the oldest, but you aren't the only one who cares. Is that why you were going to marry Angela? So you could go into business with her father?"

"It seemed like a good plan at the time. Fortunately, Angela has decided she won't marry me, but Helen thinks I can convince her otherwise."

"Well, your letter-writing exercise didn't help there."

"Thanks for that bit of useless insight. Tell me, how can I convince Helen she is the one I want and not Angela?"

"Knowing how stubborn Helen can be when she sets her mind to a thing, you shouldn't rush her. You two are friends. Continue to be her friend and pray her feelings grow into something more. I think she is already in love with you, but she isn't ready to admit it."

"I don't know. I don't have anything to offer her. No job, no business prospects. Nothing."

"What do you mean no job? I've heard Onkel Isaac tell you many times that you can stay here and work with him."

"It wouldn't be my business." Was that really so important anymore?

"That's where you're wrong. This is the family's business. You and I are already a part of it. We have been since the day we arrived."

Paul was right. God had been working on a plan for Mark's life without him even realizing it. Mark reached out and ruffled his brother's hair. "How did you get to be so smart?"

Paul playfully slapped his hand away. "Not because of anything my big brother taught me."

* * *

Helen was amazed at how easily she and Mark slipped back into old habits. He showed up for breakfast at Charlotte's three times the following week without Clyde bringing him. Sometimes she caught him staring at her with a look of longing on his face, but he would quickly look away and make a joke or tease Charlotte. On Friday, he accompanied her, along with her aunt and Clyde, to the farmers' market. Clyde and his clowning drew a crowd again, and Helen sold out of the dog biscuits before the evening was half over and took orders for another dozen packages. She was happy to stay busy because it kept her mind off how much she wanted to tell Mark about her growing feelings for him.

There was no point in denying it any longer. She was in love with him, but she couldn't say anything. She wouldn't. She had come between two people who belonged together once before and hurt them deeply in the process. She would never do anything to hurt Mark. She knew how much his plans and his family's security meant to him.

Charlotte still spent hours searching for Juliet each day. Helen had given up all hope of finding the raccoon, but Charlotte wouldn't.

Clyde remained in her room all through the night and didn't bother the Bowmans again.

On Saturday, Mark helped Helen stock her unsold items in Anna's gift shop. He carried in two large boxes for her and then stood looking around. "Where do you want these?"

"I've been putting some of the breads and rolls beside the honey and jams Anna has for sale. I put the rest of the baked goods on the table at the back."

He removed several packages of bread from her box and handed them to her to arrange to her satisfaction. "I think you should display the cookies, cake pops and dog treats beside the checkout counter. You'll get more impulse buys that way."

"You might be right." She set out the bread and headed toward the table Anna had set up for Helen's display. She moved behind the table to put a little more distance between Mark and herself.

Mark chuckled, and Helen dipped her head. She loved the sound of his laughter. "What's so funny?"

"You should have Clyde in here to point toward the dog biscuits and clown for people."

She shook her head as she put more of the goods on the table. "I don't think that's a wise idea. How many of Anna's customers would enjoy being knocked down by him?"

He planted his hands on the table and leaned toward her. She looked up and met his gaze. "Some fellas might enjoy having a pretty girl pushed into their arms. I did."

Helen felt the heat rush to her face. "I don't remember it that way."

Mark walked around the table and stood close beside her. Too close, but she couldn't move away. Every moment, it became harder to keep her feelings hidden and pretend she didn't love him. More than anything, she wanted to be held in his arms and feel the touch of his lips on hers.

"It was the loss of your cream horns that upset me." He picked up a package of them and began to unwrap it.

"Those are for sale," she said, but her voice cracked. She hoped he didn't notice.

"I'll pay for them." He took out one and bit into it but he made a sour face. "There's something wrong with these. They aren't sweet enough."

Had she made a mistake in the recipe? "Really?"

"Try a bite and see what you think." He turned the pastry around so she could sample the other end but he still held it between his fingers.

She was forced to lean forward slightly. She took a quick nibble, then pulled away. "It tastes okay to me."

He used his thumb to brush away some crumbs at the corner of her mouth. She licked her lips to remove the tingle, but it didn't help.

"I remember them being much sweeter," Mark said softly as he cupped his hand beneath her chin and leaned toward her.

Helen closed her eyes as his lips touched hers ever so softly. Her heart soared with joy. Nothing could be sweeter than this. It was everything she dreamed of and more.

The next second, he drew away. She wanted to pull him back, to know that happiness again, but the bell over the door jingled as a customer came in, forcing her return to reality. She pressed her fingers to her lips as she stared at Mark. "I'm sorry I let that happen," she whispered hoarsely.

"I'm not." The tender look in his eyes was more than she could bear.

Helen fled, leaving the rest of her goods in the boxes.

Thankfully, she was able to avoid seeing Mark on Sunday except for brief glances during the church service. She didn't stay for the lunch, giving him no opportunity to seek her out. All afternoon and evening, she waited for him to come see her at home, but he didn't. In her mind, it was proof that the kiss had been a mistake.

When Mark didn't show up for breakfast the next morning, Helen was deeply relieved. She still had no idea how she could face him or what she would say. Taking a clue from his absence, she decided the best thing to do was to pretend it never happened.

When she reached the office, she learned he would be away on business for the next several days, and she breathed a sigh of relief. She wasn't at all certain she could pull off such a pretense.

On Tuesday, the mail carrier brought Helen the letter she had been both dreading and praying to receive. It was from her family. She carried the letter down to the bank of the river to read in private. Tearing open the envelope, she pulled out a single sheet of paper. There was one line written on it.

Helen, Come home for we all love and miss you. Olivia.

Tears poured down Helen's cheeks as she clutched the letter to her chest. She loved them and missed them, too. Her shame and her pride had kept her away, but her sister's words bound up the wounds of her heart. She could go home. Maybe there, she could eventually forget about Mark and the love she didn't dare admit.

The next morning, Helen was putting out packages of cookies and cake pops to replace the ones that had sold in the gift shop. The entire Bowman family, including Mark, had gone to a picnic with Fannie's parents to celebrate Fannie's birthday, making one more day that Helen didn't have to face him. She hadn't told anyone about her plans to return home, but she would have to do so soon.

The bell over the door jingled. Helen looked up to see who had entered. It was a tall Amish woman with a wary expression on her face.

Helen smiled. "Welcome to our gift store. Feel free to look around. Be sure to ask me for help if you need it. Are you looking for something special?"

"I'm not shopping. I hoped you could tell me where I might find Mark Bowman. I've been to the house, but no one is there, and the business seems to be closed until later today."

"Mark and his family have gone on a picnic with the Erb family. It's a birthday party for their daughter, but he should back before long. Is he expecting you? I can give you directions to the Erb farm."

"Mark isn't expecting me. In fact, I'm sure he'll be shocked to see me. I'll just wait, if that's okay." She carried a small suitcase in one hand, and Helen wondered who she was.

"Of course. You are welcome to wait here, or you can go over to the house and wait there. The Bowmans won't mind. I'm Helen Zook. I'm a neighbor."

The woman smiled. "It's nice to meet you, Helen. I'm Angela Yoder."

Helen stared at her in shock. "From Pennsylvania?"

"I take it Mark has mentioned me."

"He has." What did Angela want? Why had she come all this way to see Mark when he was returning to Pennsylvania in another few weeks?

"I'm on my way to a cousin's wedding in Millersburg, and I had my driver stop here since I was this close. I wasn't expecting to wait. I can't stay long."

"I'm sure Mark will be delighted to see you."

"I hope so. I sure do hope so," Angela muttered more to herself than to Helen. "What has he said about me?"

"That you and he had an understanding but that you changed your mind."

Angela's laugh sounded flat. "I guess he has told you quite a bit. You must know him well."

"We're friends."

"That's more than I can say, and I'm going to marry him."

Helen's heart plunged to her feet. She should be glad for him, but all she felt was heartbreak. "Mark is a fine man. He is honest and hardworking. He will make a loving and comforting husband. He deserves to be happy, and so do you."

"I hope what I have to tell him will make us both happy."

Mark's letter must have convinced her to give him another chance. "His dream of a business back home means everything to him."

"I'm glad to know that."

Helen noticed the Bowmans' buggy turn in and stop. Mark and Anna got out, but Isaac and the others drove on. "Here he comes now."

The bell over the door jangled as Mark and his aunt entered. Anna pulled off her black traveling bonnet. "I'm ever so grateful that you kept an eye on things here, Helen, but you are free to go now." She went behind the counter and hung up her bonnet.

Mark had seen Angela. He looked frozen in place. Angela walked toward him. "Hello, Mark."

"Angela! What are you doing here?"

Angela glanced around nervously. "I wanted to see you. I've made a mistake. Is there somewhere private that we can talk?"

He glanced at Helen. She turned away to finish filling the shelf and to hide the tears pricking the backs of her eyes.

"Angela, if you will step across to the wood-working shop, I'll be over in a few minutes and we can talk in my office. I need to speak to Helen first."

"Okay." Angela glanced between them but went out the door.

"Don't keep her waiting, Mark. She came a long way. Your letter convinced her to change her mind." Helen moved farther down the counter.

"Helen, please. I want to tell you how much you have come to mean to me."

She turned around with a bright smile frozen in place. "Your friendship has meant the world to me, too."

"I think we both know this is more than friendship between us, Helen. I haven't forgotten our kiss."

Neither had she. She drew a deep breath

and faced him. "I've had a letter from my sister asking me to come home. I'm going."

He frowned. "When did you decide this?"

"After I read my sister's letter. I've been very selfish. I didn't realize how much my leaving hurt everyone. I need to reconcile with her and the rest of my family."

"Then you'll come back?"

She saw the hope in his eyes and couldn't bear it. If he gave up his dream for her, she would always regret causing that. "*Nee.* Nappanee is my home. That's where I belong."

"What about Charlotte?"

"She is tired of having me in the house. She'll do fine. She has friends and the church to look after her."

"When are you leaving?"

"The soonest I can get a bus home is Saturday."

"What about us?" he asked softly.

She sighed deeply and turned to him. "You and I will always be friends. I hope you'll write and tell me how the business is doing and if your father is enjoying working with you."

He stepped up to grasp her shoulders. "I thought we had something special."

"We had a special friendship. I'm sorry if you thought it was something more. Go to Angela. You have everything you've dreamed of now." She pulled away and fled out the door before she could blurt out that she loved him.

Mark watched Helen leave as a wave of sorrow nearly brought him to his knees. He should have found a way to make her stay and listen to him. He should have told her sooner how much he loved her and how much he wanted her to be a part of his life. How could she not love him in return? How could she walk away? Bereft as much now as he had been as a child, he blinked back tears.

Maybe he shouldn't have kissed her.

No, if nothing else, he would have that one sweet memory to carry with him forever.

"I'm sorry, Mark." He'd forgotten Anna was still there until she spoke.

"She doesn't love me. Am I so hard to love? What's wrong with me?"

Anna came and put her arms around him, pulling him close to comfort him as she had when he was a small scared boy. "Many people love you. *Gott* loves you. Never doubt that."

"What should I do?"

"Give Helen some time and then go speak her, and tell her how you feel."

"How much time? You heard her. She's

leaving on Saturday." What if she didn't love him? How could he face that?

Anna held him at arm's length. "Silly boy. You can always buy a ticket to Indiana, too. These things happen in *Gott's* time. Have faith."

He closed his eyes. *Please, Lord, show me how to make her see that I love her.*

He gave his aunt a weak smile. "I reckon I should go speak with Angela."

"You do that. Close one door and perhaps a new door will open more easily."

Mark left his aunt's gift shop and crossed the parking lot to the woodworking shop. He found Angela seated in his small office. A faint frown creased her brow. She didn't look happy to see him. How had he ever imagined being married to her? "I'm sorry I took so long."

"I should have let you know I was coming."

"If you had, I might have been able to save you the trip. I won't marry you, Angela. Your father may keep his land and the money I have paid him if he feels I have broken our contract, but I love someone else."

Angela closed her eyes, clasped her hands to her chest and lifted her face to the ceiling. "Thank you, dearest Lord, for hearing my prayers."

Mark wasn't sure what to make of her words. "I thought you had come to tell me you would marry me."

She drew a deep breath and looked at him. "I did."

"Then I'm confused."

"Father has been pressuring me to accept you ever since I told you I had changed my mind. I finally gave in only to learn his insistence wasn't because he wanted me to be happy. He didn't want to return your money."

"Let him keep it."

She smiled. "*Nee*, for it is yours. This has been a lesson to my father on the sin of greed. We have not spent a penny of it. I have brought the full amount with me in case you did not wish to marry me."

She opened her purse, pulled out a bank draft and held it toward him. "Father wasn't happy to write this check, but he has seen the error of his ways."

Mark slowly took it from her. "Won't your father be upset?"

She grinned, giving him a glimpse of a woman he hadn't seen before. "I'm sure he will be, but I'm his only child. He'll forgive me in time. I'm on my way to my cousin's wedding and since you won't have me, I will be able to have a wedding of my own soon.

My late husband's best friend, Anthony, has offered for me. Now I'm free to say yes. My father can't interfere or forbid it. Anthony is a good man, but he isn't fond of my father. He wants us to move to Colorado."

"Will you go?"

"Happily. Daed will be free to visit us whenever he likes."

Mark shook his head. "What would you have done if I had agreed to marry you?"

"Spent my life being a good wife to you."

"We would have both been miserable."

"Maybe, maybe not. Only God knows that, but He had a better plan for us. I have to get going. I have a driver waiting for me."

Mark stood and held out his hand. "I wish you every happiness."

She leaned in and kissed his cheek. "I pray the same for you. What will you do now?"

He would give Helen some time, but he was going to speak to her before she left Bowmans Crossing. "I'm going to follow my heart and see where it and God lead me."

Chapter Fourteen

The following morning, Helen was on her way to tell Isaac about her decision and say good-bye to the people she had worked with in the shop. It would be hard to see Mark again, but she could bear it knowing things had worked out for him and he would be happy in the life he had worked so hard to achieve. Charlotte had insisted on coming with her to visit Anna again. Clyde, her ever-present shadow, lay on the floor snoring.

Helen heard the sound of a chainsaw as she approached the covered bridge. The sound echoed inside the bridge structure, making her horse twitch his ears nervously. Clyde sat up and began barking furiously. He struggled against the hold Charlotte had on his collar.

"What is the matter with you?" Charlotte

asked the dog as she got a better grip on him. He squirmed harder.

When Helen came out the other side of the bridge, she saw Mark and his uncle standing beneath Clyde's tree. Several large limbs lay on the ground already. Paul was up in the tree itself with the chainsaw. She pulled her horse to a stop off the edge of the road to watch.

Paul, secured with a harness and rope, was cutting through a large dead limb that hung toward the river. From her vantage point, she saw something the foliage of the tree had kept hidden until now. There was a large knot hole in the middle of the dead limb. To her amazement, a raccoon stuck its head out of the hole and then vanished back inside. "Aenti, did you see that?"

"See what?" Charlotte bent forward for a better view.

Helen had only a momentary glimpse of the animal. "I'm sure I saw a raccoon, and I think I saw a flash of pink on its neck."

"Do you mean you saw Juliet? The Lord be praised."

The raccoon's hideaway was about to plummet twenty feet to the ground. Helen leaped from her buggy waving her arms. "Stop! Wait!"

Clyde's struggles and yelping grew frenzied. He broke away from Charlotte and raced toward the men.

The workers didn't hear Helen's shouts over the loud buzz of the saw. She got out of the buggy and rushed down the steep embankment, struggling to keep her balance as she continued yelling. Clyde caught Mark's attention by jumping on him, but it was too late. The saw stopped as the huge limb toppled out of the tree, hit the ground and then rolled down into the river. Clyde raced after it and plunged into the water.

Helen stopped her mad dash and pressed a hand to her heart, certain that she had just watched Juliet's demise.

"Clyde, come back," Charlotte shouted as she followed Helen down the slope. "Mark, help him. Basset hounds are terrible swimmers. He'll drown."

Juliet scrambled out of the hole. She held a kit in her mouth. After pacing back and forth for several seconds, she left the log and began swimming for shore. Clyde tried to change direction and follow her, but he was struggling badly. When he went under, Charlotte screamed.

Mark rushed to the water's edge, pulled off his boots, threw his hat aside and dived into the water. He came up, swimming toward the spot where Clyde had vanished. To Helen's relief, the dog surfaced, although he was clearly fading. Mark reached him and tried to support him. It was all he could do to keep Clyde's head above water.

Helen saw a rowboat beached near the bridge. She raced to it, pushed off and got in. Rowing was not as easy as it looked, but she managed to turn the boat and headed toward Mark. She pulled alongside them, shipped the oars and leaned over to grab Clyde's collar.

"I've got him." As soon as she took his weight, the boat tipped dangerously.

"Don't let him pull you in," Mark shouted. "Can you swim?"

"I never learned."

"The time to learn is before you are in danger of falling into the river."

"Thanks for the tip," she said through gritted teeth. Her arms ached from holding Clyde's weight as he continued to struggle.

Mark grasped the rope at the bow of the boat and began towing it to shore.

They were within a few feet of the bank. Paul, Isaac and Charlotte stood on dry ground calling encouragement and instructions, but Helen was barely holding on. Clyde gave a sudden, powerful lunge. The boat tipped, spilling Helen over the side. She shrieked as she hit the cold water and sank. Seconds later, strong arms grasped her and pulled her to the surface. She came up choking and sputtering.

"I've got you. You're fine," Mark said calmly.

She clutched him tightly, afraid they were both about to die. "I can't swim."

"You don't have to swim, my love. Put your feet down. It's not that deep here."

She realized he was right. She could touch the bottom. Mark captured one of her hands and led her toward the shore. Clyde bounded out and shook himself off before lumbering to where Juliet was licking her kit. She greeted Clyde with a warning hiss, then relented and began licking him, too. Charlotte dropped to her knees to stroke Juliet's head. The raccoon reached up and patted her face. Charlotte was crying tears of joy.

Isaac and Paul reached Helen and Mark as they emerged from the water. "Are you two okay?" Isaac asked.

Helen nodded and sank to the ground. Mark sat beside her. She looked at his beloved face and wished he would take her in his arms. She loved him so much, but he belonged to Angela.

She let her fright turn to anger so she wouldn't blurt out her secret. "Mark Bowman, that was the stupidest thing I've ever seen a man do. That dog could have pulled you under. Was that the plan?"

He grinned at her. "I didn't have a plan. I just went with my heart. The boat was a better idea. *Danki*, my darling, but if we are going to live by this river, you and our children are going to learn to swim."

Her mouth dropped open. What did he mean? Before she could gather her scattered wits to ask, Anna arrived and draped a quilt around her. "You poor dear. Come up to the house and get out of those wet clothes before you catch your death."

Isaac pointed to the river, where the tree limb was caught at the edge of the bridge and bobbing in the current. A second tiny raccoon kit had crawled out of the hole and was crying. If the limb became dislodged it would be swept downriver.

Mark looked up at Paul. Paul nodded. "Let's try."

Mark rose to his feet. Helen caught hold of his pant leg. "Try what?"

He loosened her hand and gave it a squeeze. "We need to rescue the rest of Juliet's family." He and Paul pushed the boat out and climbed in.

Helen scrambled to her feet and pulled the quilt more tightly around her shoulders. Anna steadied her with an arm around her waist. They all watched silently as the two men maneuvered the boat up beside the log. If it became dislodged, it could easily overturn the boat. Unable to reach the opening where two little masked faces were staring at them, Mark slipped over the side of the skiff and into the water. Helen pressed a hand to her mouth to keep from crying out.

Mark pulled himself in among the branches and reached into the cavity. One by one, he pulled out three babies and handed them to Paul. Before Mark could get back to the boat, the limb broke free of the piling and rolled as the current swept it underneath the bridge, taking Mark with it. Helen screamed.

Chapter Fifteen

Helen dropped the quilt and ran toward the base of the bridge with Isaac and Anna close behind her. She heard Paul shouting for Mark. The tree limb bobbed faster in the swift current between the bridge pilings and disappeared from her sight. She closed her eyes. "Please, Lord, spare his life. I love him so much. Please be merciful."

She could hear Paul shouting, and then there was silence. She stared into the dark shadows under the bridge and prayed as she had never prayed in her life. Then she saw the bow of the boat emerging into the light. Paul was rowing with difficulty against the current. Finally, the rest of the boat appeared with Mark sitting at the rear.

Helen's knees gave way, and she sat abruptly in the grass as tears of joy and thanksgiving blurred her vision. Anna and Isaac helped her to her feet. "He's fine," Anna said. "He's fine. Praise God for His goodness." There was as much relief in her voice as there was in Helen's heart.

Paul beached the boat and both men climbed out. Paul scooped the mewing kits from the floor of the boat and carried them to their mother. She took each one, nosed it thoroughly and then licked it before she seemed satisfied. Helen had never seen her aunt looking so happy, as she gathered the new family into her apron.

Mark sat beside Helen and leaned close to whisper in her ear. "At least we know why he was always barking beneath the tree."

Nodding, Helen smiled at him. "He was trying to convince her to come home."

There was so much more she wanted to say to him, but she settled for whispering, "Thank you."

He smiled softly. "You're welcome."

Helen's gaze shifted to the house. "I hope Angela didn't see this."

"She's not here. She's gone to her cousin's wedding."

"Oh." She didn't know what else to say. All through the previous sleepless night she had practice telling him goodbye and wishing him well without bursting into tears. It would be impossible at the moment for tears were already gathering in her eyes. She blinked them back.

Clyde crawled close beside Charlotte, who was sitting cross-legged on the grass, and laid his head on her knee as he gazed at the pile of babies. Charlotte patted his head. "You will make a fine stepfather. Oh, what fun we shall have."

Anna made shooing motions at Mark and Helen. "Up to the house, both of you, and get out of those wet things."

Helen allowed herself to be shepherded up to the house, where she changed into clothing borrowed from Rebecca. By the time she came down to the living room, word of the morning's adventure had spread. Mark and Paul were surrounded by the men from the workshop asking questions and shaking their heads in amazement.

Anna came out of the kitchen and stopped beside Helen. "Charlotte is anxious to get home and get Juliet and her family settled into a safer nest."

Helen had her battered emotions under control. She wanted to speak with Mark, to say her goodbyes but not in front of everyone. He looked up and caught sight of her. He made his way through his friends to her side. "Are you okay?"

No, she wasn't. Her heart was breaking, but she managed a half-hearted smile. "A little waterlogged. I'm going to have to wash my hair."

He grinned at her. "Then you're going be home this evening?"

"Most definitely."

His brother Joshua came in with his wife, Mary, and their daughter, Hannah. "I've been hearing that my cousin jumped in the river to save a raccoon. Is it true?"

Mark tipped his head close to Helen. "I'll be over to see you in a couple of hours. I have a lot of things to tell you."

He turned to his cousin, and Helen's smile faded. All she had to say to him was goodbye.

Mark couldn't wait until evening. It was only four thirty when he stepped onto Charlotte's front porch with a package under one arm. His heart was pounding in his chest. Could he convince Helen that he loved her? Would she give him a chance to prove his love, or was her mind still set on leaving? Did she love him even a little or was he only fooling himself? He loved her so much. The thought of going through life without her was unbearable.

He knocked on the door, but no one answered. Had she changed her mind about seeing him?

Clyde ambled around from the side of the house and woofed once. He turned around and went back the way he had come. Mark took it as an invitation to follow him. He hadn't been in Charlotte's flower garden during daylight hours.

He stepped through a white lattice arbor laden with fragrant red roses. Helen was seated on a white wrought-iron bench in the middle of a stone patio, surrounded by yellow and purple irises. She hadn't seen him. She was brushing her unbound hair. She looked to be enjoying the feel of the warm sun on her face. Her wheat-blond hair glistened in the sunlight and shimmered like liquid gold with each stroke of her brush. He sucked in his breath as he realized she was truly a pearl beyond price, but her beauty wasn't the reason he loved her. He loved every complicated and fascinating part of her mind. Every giggle, every frown, every sigh. He wanted to have and to hold her for all eternity. If she loved him.

Clyde nudged the back of Mark's knee. He looked down at the dog. "I'm going, I'm going."

Helen must've heard him for she opened her eyes and turned her head toward him. The happiness he saw in her beautiful eyes left him speechless. How could he have imagined spending a lifetime with a wife he didn't love?

Helen quickly looked away as the joy in her expression turned to sadness. His confidence slipped. Maybe she didn't love him.

She looked up and shook her hairbrush at him. "You're early."

"Shall I go away and come back later?"

"*Nee*, you should come and sit beside me."

"I reckon that's the best invitation I'm liable to get all day."

She scooted over to make room for him. He sat down, suddenly tongue-tied and nervous. She fiddled with the brush in her hands and avoided looking at him. Clyde decided to sit on the bench beside her, forcing Helen to scoot closer to Mark.

Knowing the dog was on his side, Mark's courage returned. "I brought you something." He handed her the package.

She took it from him, held it to her ear and shook it. The rattle of glass made her eyes widen. "What is this for? It's not my birthday."

"I'll explain in a minute."

"What is it?"

"Open it and see."

She quickly tore off the brown paper wrapping and gasped. Gently, she ran her fingers over the figures of Clyde in various poses, sitting, rolling over, sleeping, even flying with his ears out straight, all carved in relief into the dark walnut doors. She opened the doors and pulled out one of the dozen empty spice jars.

"I didn't put the labels on because I didn't know what spices you would want," he said quickly, hoping she liked it.

She tucked the jar back in place and closed the doors. "Mark, this is beautiful. But why?"

"I'm hoping it's an engagement gift. Helen Zook, will you do me the honor of becoming my wife?"

Her mouth dropped open. "You can't mean that. You're going to marry Angela."

"I'm not."

"You aren't? What about the land and the business? You've spent years working to fulfill your plans. I don't understand."

"The good Lord has opened my eyes and made me see that my plan wasn't His plan for me. You are if you will have me. I'm not much, but I promise to be a good and loving husband. Will you marry me?"

"You're not going to marry Angela?"

"*Nee*, I'm not."

"You're not going to start a business with her father?"

"Nope."

Her eyes widened as his words sank in. "Why?"

"Because I love you. Do you…do you care for me at all?" He held his breath.

"Oh, Mark I love you, too. I can't believe this is happening. I have been rehearsing how to say goodbye without falling apart."

"God willing I will never hear that speech." He laid the spice rack aside, pulled her close and kissed her as every fiber of his being shouted with joy. After a long interval, he pulled away to look into her eyes.

"I love you, Helen Zook. I think I fell in love with you when you smashed those delicious cream horns into my chest."

She covered her face with her hands and laughed. "I was absolutely humiliated that day. The look on your face did not say *I love you*."

He took her hands in his. "What does the look on my face say today?"

Tenderness filled her eyes. "It says everything I have always wanted to hear."

He swept back a lock of her hair. "Does it say 'I think you are beautiful?'"

She tipped her head to the side to study him. "I believe it does."

He gently cupped her face and ran his thumb across her lips. "Does it say that I'm dying to kiss you again?"

She tipped her head slightly. "I don't see that in your eyes."

"Then I reckon I had better show you." He bent forward and gently kissed her.

She sighed against his lips. He turned to gather her in his arms and draw her close. Her arms circled his neck, and he thought his heart might explode with the love that expanded inside him. Her lips were soft and yielding beneath his. He'd never know a sweeter moment in his life. He kissed her eyelids and her cute nose and the pulse beating in her throat.

When she finally drew back, he knew without a doubt that this was the woman God meant to be his wife. "I didn't know I could love someone so much," he whispered.

"It came as a surprise to me, too," she said with a smile. "God has been good to us."

"What is your answer, woman of my heart?"

Helen grew somber as she gazed at the man she loved. "In answer to your earlier question, *ja*, Mark Bowman, I will be pleased to become your wife. This morning you said that we will raise our children by this river. Have you decided not to return to Pennsylvania?"

"I've been working on a new plan, but I'm going to need some help with it."

"I'm always willing to give you *my* point of view."

He kissed the tip of her nose. "Even when I don't want it, I know. This time, I want it. I've taken some inspiration from you. You love baking, and it shows in what you produce. The part I like best about building furniture is carving. I'm a good carver. I think I can become a master carver in time. Adam Knepp, my uncle's master carver, is willing to teach me. My uncle says I have the gift. Bowmans Crossing is drawing more tourists every year. I think a bakery beside the gift shop can become a paying proposition in two or three years with the right baker in charge."

"Me? You want me to have my own bakery?" She shook her head sadly. "We don't have the money for that."

"When I told Angela I couldn't marry her, she gave me back the money I had paid to her father. She was hoping I wouldn't take her back. Her father pressured her into saying that she had reconsidered and that she was willing to go through with our arrangement, but she wanted to marry someone else. She didn't come because of the letter you thought I wrote her. I never sent it. I was writing it to you. I wanted to hear what it would take to make you love me."

Helen laid a hand on his cheek. She was glad he hadn't sent Angela that letter. "Are you sure about this? You dreamed of owning your own business there for so many years."

He covered her hand with his and turned to place a kiss on her palm. "God has given me a new dream. One that will change and grow over time as He blesses us with children and grandchildren."

"I like the sound of that."

He kissed her temple. "So do I. When can we wed?"

"As soon as the banns are announced is fine with me," Helen said and leaned toward him for another kiss.

"Nonsense," Charlotte declared from her bedroom window. "Fall is the time for weddings. You don't want folks wondering why the rush. We have so much to do to get ready. Are you finished wooing yet?"

"Not yet, Charlotte," Mark said sternly. "Stop eavesdropping, and shut your window."

"How rude. Helen was right about you." She slammed the window sash down with a bang.

Clyde woofed. Mark looked over at him. "Get lost. I've got this."

The dog jumped down from the bench and trotted around the corner of the house.

"Now, where was I?" Mark asked, gathering Helen close once more.

She tapped her lips with one finger. "I think you were here."

"I believe you're right."

Helen thrilled to the touch of his lips on hers and proceeded to kiss him with all the passion in her heart. God had indeed been good to them.

* * * * *

If you enjoyed
AN UNEXPECTED AMISH ROMANCE,
look for the other books in the
AMISH BACHELORS series:

AN AMISH HARVEST
AN AMISH NOEL
HIS AMISH TEACHER
THEIR PRETEND AMISH COURTSHIP
AMISH CHRISTMAS TWINS

Dear Readers

I have both a cat and a dog and I love them both, but my dog loves me back while my cat only likes me. Clyde is the combination of several dogs that I have owned. While none of them have been basset hounds, they shared some of the clownish behavior that is characteristic of the breed. Bumper, a Boston terrier, was a true clown. He would sing along while my husband played his accordion, and he would torment our cat.

Kahn, a massive black Lab, could knock you off your feet without a second thought. He was always sorry and would cover your face with kisses before you could get to your feet. He was also noted for licking my ear while I was driving. Not often, but it was distracting when it happened.

Gertie, a shepherd mix, would vanish at night and show up the next morning with a gift for me. Usually, it was a stick of firewood, cut and cured. I'd add it to our woodpile and thank her. Once, she brought me a pair of men's underwear. We lived out in the country, and our nearest neighbor was a half mile away. I did not try to return the briefs. I sure wished she could tell me that story.

Sadie was a yellow Lab-and-pointer mix who owned our hearts for nine beautiful years. She had pussy-willow ears—long and softer than silk. I believe she understood everything we said. She had the amazing ability to do what we asked with happy, loving energy. I miss her greatly.

I believe our pets are angels sent from God to lighten the burdens of our lives and to show us truly unconditional love. As I am writing this, Sugar, my rat terrier mix, is watching me from the bed. She naps while I write but if I get up and put on my shoes, she becomes a bouncing ball of energy. She knows I'm going outside.

I hope you enjoyed meeting Clyde and Juliet as well as Helen and Mark. Charlotte will remain one of my favorite characters of all time. Thanks for letting me tell you another tale about the Bowman family. Paul's story will be next. I'm searching for the perfect girl for him right now.

Blessings,

Patricia Davids